Coming to Rosemont
by
BARBARA HINSKE

CreateSpace

Coming to Rosemont

COPYRIGHT 2011 BARBARA HINSKE

www.barbarahinske.com

ISBN-13: 978-1481125277
ISBN-10: 1481125273

CreateSpace
Charleston, SC

Dedication

To my remarkable parents, who instilled in me every high ideal and greater instinct I've ever had, to my incredible husband for his sage advice and unshakeable support, and to my legion of extraordinary friends whose examples inspire me.

Prologue

Frank Haynes spotted the forlorn-looking creature in the trees at the side of the road. He quickly pulled his Mercedes sedan off the highway and buttoned his cashmere sport coat against the icy fog as he stepped out onto the grassy berm. He walked gingerly in his slick-bottomed dress shoes as he approached the thin calico lurking in the underbrush. The wary animal rose up on her front legs, ready to take flight, and eyed him uneasily.

Haynes crooned softly to her. He pulled his collar up against the biting wind and wished he had grabbed his topcoat out of the backseat. But he dare not move now. She gradually relaxed and cautiously picked her way to him over the frost-stiffened grass. The cat rubbed against his legs in the familiar figure-eight pattern and began to purr – a tiny, tentative whisper that ripened into a deep, throaty rumble.

He reached a cautious hand down to her. She stretched into him and he knew the bond had been made. He scooped her up and cradled the filthy creature against his chest, shielding her from the cold and stroking her gently, unconcerned about his expensive coat. When she was content, he returned to his car and placed her carefully in the blanket-lined crate that lived in his backseat for just such occasions. "You're safe now," he whispered the assurance. "You won't have to worry about food or cold anymore."

He shut the mesh grate on the cage and was surprised that the cat curled up and went to sleep. Most strays meowed and screamed all the way to the no-kill shelter that Haynes had founded and currently funded.

As he slipped behind the steering wheel, Haynes automatically checked the cell phone left behind in the console and was surprised to see he missed six calls during the short time he had been rescuing the cat. All from their idiot Mayor, William Wheeler. He punched the return call button as he swung back onto the highway. Wheeler picked up on the first ring.

"Christ, Frank, where the hell have you been? All hell's going to break loose around here," Wheeler shouted into the phone.

"What's up?" Haynes replied calmly.

"The Town Treasurer just called and told me the Town can't cover the December payments from the pension fund. Jesus, Frank."

Shit, Haynes thought. This is coming two months earlier than he predicted. Damn. We won't have time to get any of those condos sold by December. "Have you talked to either of the Delgados?"

"I called Chuck to tell him to move money from the reserve account you guys told me about. He said to talk to Ron about it. Ron thinks the reserve account has been 'depleted.' Some accountant and financial advisor he is! How did you guys let this happen? What have you been up to? If the Town doesn't make those payments, the shit will hit the fan."

"Don't worry about it. I'll call Chuck and we'll get it straightened out. We always do, don't we?" Haynes disconnected the call over Wheeler's sputtering response.

Damn this faltering real estate market and those greedy, careless Delgado brothers. How had they drained the reserve fund so quickly? They must be siphoning money for their own use from the tidy sum that the three of them had "borrowed" from the Town Worker's Pension Fund. Fleecing the faceless public was one thing. Double-crossing Frank Haynes was quite another. Wheeler was set up to take the fall, if it came to that. He could make the trail lead to the Delgados, too. Haynes vowed to find out where every nickel had gone. He executed a sharp U-turn and headed back to Town Hall.

Chapter 1

Maggie Martin settled herself in the back of the cab as the driver pulled away from the airport and into the thin sunshine of a late February afternoon. She nodded mutely when he leaned back to tell her that Westbury was an hour's drive and turned her attention to the countryside streaming by her window. She was in no mood for idle chatter with a taxi driver. The dormant farmland lay still and expectant. Occasional clumps of leafless trees were silhouetted against the storm clouds that soon filled the sky. Maggie was glad she had carefully folded and packed those extra sweaters.

She shivered in spite of the heat blasting from the vents and wondered idly how anyone could live in a cold climate. Southern California might not have four seasons, but who in their right mind wanted winter? Maggie chastised herself once again for even making this trip. She was behind in her work – she needed the billings – and she probably wouldn't find any answers, anyway.

As the monotonous scenery sped by, Maggie relived her final moments with Paul. He was in the cardiac ICU, wired, tubed, and hooked up to the best equipment modern medicine had to offer. Mike and Susan were both frantically making their way through traffic, but neither arrived in time. It had been Maggie and Paul at the very end. In his final moments, Paul rallied. He feebly squeezed Maggie's hand and repeated breathlessly, "Sorry. So sorry. House is for you." At least, that's what Maggie thought he said. She had been crying and the beeping monitors and wheezing oxygen machine made it impossible to hear.

She had been over this a million times. It hadn't made any sense because she knew their house was hers. Hadn't they just paid it off and thrown a burn-the-mortgage party with the kids? She had tried to reassure Paul, to quiet him, but he had been desperate to make his point. Maggie now understood Paul's deathbed confession. That's why she had to come to Rosemont before she listed it for sale. She needed to get answers; to make some sense of her life.

Maggie had planned to go straight to her hotel in Westbury to try to get a good night's sleep before she and the realtor toured the house and signed the listing papers the next day. But her plane had arrived forty-five minutes early, the only advantage of the bumpy flight through strong tailwinds. God knows she was exhausted, having spent another sleepless night rehashing her sham of a marriage. But she was far too curious to get a glimpse of Rosemont to wait any longer. As they passed the highway sign announcing the Westbury exit in fourteen miles, Maggie retrieved her house key from the zippered compartment of her purse, leaned forward, and instructed the driver to take her directly to Rosemont.

The cabbie, as it turned out, didn't need directions. "Everybody in these parts knows the place," he assured her. "It's been vacant for years," he continued as he caught her eye in his rearview mirror. "Do you know the owner?" he asked.

"I am the owner," Maggie replied with an assurance in her voice that surprised her. "Actually, I just inherited Rosemont. I'm going to put it on the market, but I'm awfully curious to see it. Since it'll still be light when we get there, I thought I'd like to see it on my own, before the realtor and I get together tomorrow."

The cabbie nodded slowly, digesting this news, as he flipped on his left-turn signal and turned into a long, tree-lined drive that wound its way up a steep hill. They rounded the final corner and Maggie gasped. At the end of a deep lawn was an elegant manor house of aristocratic proportions. Built of warm limestone, with regal multi-paned windows, a sharply-pitched tile roof, and six chimneys, Rosemont had the kind of gracious good looks that never go out of style. Dazed, she handed him his fare, with a more-than-generous tip, and secured his promise to drop her luggage at her hotel and return for her in an hour.

Maggie dashed through the now-falling sleet to the massive front door. The key fit smoothly into the lock but wouldn't turn. She tugged and jiggled the handle, to no effect. It wasn't moving. Maggie looked wistfully over her shoulder as the taxi took the last turn at the end of the drive and vanished into the trees. Damn it – why did she have to insist on coming here tonight? Impatience did her in every time.

She buttoned the top button of her coat, fished the cabbie's card out of her pocket, and unzipped her purse to retrieve her phone. She'd have to call him to come back now. It was too cold and damp to even walk around outside and look in the windows. Maggie tugged off one of her gloves with her teeth and punched in his number on her phone. She brought it to her ear and idly tried the lock one more time. She felt something shift under her hand and the sturdy lock yielded. The door creaked open. Maggie abruptly ended the call and stepped over the threshold.

Even in the gloomy light of a stormy dusk, the beauty of the house overwhelmed Maggie and she knew, for perhaps the first time in her life, that she was home. And that nothing would ever be the same again.

The mahogany front door opened to a foyer that gave way to a generous living room. A stone fireplace with an ornately-carved mantle dominated one side of the room and a graceful stairway swept up the opposite wall to the second floor. An archway led to a room lined with bookcases. An honest-to-goodness library, for Pete's sake, Maggie thought.

She inched forward slowly, as if expecting to come to the end of her leash, and peered into the library. Although all of the furniture was draped in heavy muslin covers, the room was stunning with its six-foot-high fireplace, French doors to a patio, and a stained-glass window. "I've been transported to a movie set of an English manor house," Maggie whispered.

She set her purse on a round table in the middle of the foyer and unbuttoned her coat. The fatigue and apathy that had been Maggie's constant companions since Paul's death began to dissipate as Maggie examined this elegant old house she had inherited. Paul had never mentioned owning an estate on fifteen acres in Westbury. At least not until his final moments. Maggie had learned a lot of things that Paul had never mentioned. Unlike the others, this one was a pleasant surprise.

The remainder of the first floor was comprised of a large dining room, butler's pantry, kitchen, breakfast room, laundry, maid's quarters, and a large, sunny room whose function she couldn't identify. It had a herringbone tile floor and was lined with floor-to-ceiling windows along one wall. A conservatory, maybe? Holy cow – did she actually own a home with a library and a conservatory? The perfect lines of the house were evident at every turn.

With mounting excitement, Maggie found the switch for the chandelier that lit the staircase and raced to the second floor. A spacious landing gave way to six separate bedroom suites. She opened the first door carefully and proceeded with increasing confidence. Each suite was lovely and distinct in its own way, with huge windows and a sitting room and bathroom for each bedroom. One had a balcony; two had fireplaces. "I actually own this place," she murmured to herself in shock. She was considering which bedroom she liked best when she thought she heard a door close below. Was it already time for the taxi to return for her? Could she possibly have been here for an hour?

Maggie tore down the stairs as surely as if she had been running down them all of her life and came face to face with a solidly-built man wearing tidy work clothes. With a pounding heart but steady voice, Maggie demanded to know who he was and how he got into her house.

He stepped back and held up his hands,. "I'm sorry to startle you, ma'am. I'm Sam Torres. Your realtor expected you day-after-tomorrow and asked me to come by today to air the house out a bit and make sure that everything was in working order. I've been in the basement for the past three hours fiddling with the furnace. I've got it going now. I'm surprised we didn't hear each other. I didn't mean to frighten you." He paused a moment to wipe his hands on a rag. He was never very good at guessing ages; he figured she must be in her fifties, but couldn't tell which end of that age range she leaned to. She was wrapped in a down-filled coat and wore those enormous Australian boots that were so popular. His wife lived in hers from October to May. She had a pair of glasses perched on her nose and was now regarding him imperiously through these.

"Welcome to Rosemont," he continued. "I understand you plan to put it on the market right away?"

Something about his polite, calm manner put her immediately at ease. Judging by his weathered skin and full head of grey hair, he must be a few years her senior. She extended her hand to introduce herself and indicated that she was most definitely not going to sell this place. To her own astonishment, she announced "As soon as my taxi returns I'm going to check out of my hotel and move in here. Tonight. Permanently."

Sam looked at her sharply and started to reply, but stopped himself. She reached for the banister, as if to steady herself, and turned aside. What are you doing, she thought to herself. You can't just up and move here. Are you nuts? What do you need with a six-bedroom house? Your family is in California, and so is your work. Maggie glanced back; the man was regarding her carefully. She wondered if he could sense that her decision to move into the house that night had been made, impetuously, on the spot.

"In that case," he continued, "I'd better give you a complete tour. You'll need to know where all the entrances, switches and thermostats are located." He gestured toward the library and began by showing her how to unlock and open the cantankerous old French doors. Sam nodded in the direction of the fireplace. "You won't want to start a fire until all of these chimneys have been cleaned and checked. This house hasn't been lived in for more than a decade." Sam paused and turned to Maggie. "Are you sure you want to move in here tonight? Once the plumbing is in use again, you'll find almost everything leaks. And the place hasn't been cleaned in years. Wouldn't you like to get it fixed up first?"

"No, I can live with all of that for a few days. As long as the furnace works and the electricity and water are turned on, I can cope."

"This sleet is supposed to turn to snow. You might get stranded up here." He cautioned as he produced a business card for *Sam the Handyman*. "Here's my card. My cell phone number is on there. Why don't you call me when you get back tonight and

I can stop by to make sure that the furnace is still running and you're all set?" he offered.

"Thank you – very kind of you – but no need to drag out here later. I'll be fine," Maggie assured him with a confidence she didn't feel. For some reason, she felt completely comfortable with this concerned stranger. "Truthfully, this is a rash decision on my part." Sam nodded. "I can't explain it. I've never done anything like this in my entire life. But every fiber of my being tells me this is the right thing to do. For once in my adult life, I'm going to follow my intuition."

Sam regarded Maggie intently and a slow smile lightened his worried expression. "In that case, moving in is exactly what you should do. Sounds like divine intuition. You should follow it. And you can always call me if anything comes up. My wife and I live about ten minutes away."

"Thank you, Sam. That makes me feel more comfortable." They resumed their tour and Maggie was secretly relieved that Sam made sure all the windows and doors were locked and all the thermostats were set. His instructions were thorough and helpful. It was evident that he knew the house well. The first floor had warmed to room temperature by the time they returned to the front door.

"I appreciate all you've done," Maggie said. "I'm not a dab hand at home repairs, so I'm sure I'll need your help on a regular basis. What do I owe you for today" she asked as she turned toward her purse.

"Don't worry about that now" Sam said as he reached for the door "We can settle up later. Would you like me to have the driveway plowed tomorrow?" She gratefully accepted as they said goodnight and he headed out the door.

Later, in the eerie brightness of the nighttime snowstorm, Maggie and the taxi driver wrestled her suitcases and three bags of groceries to her front door. The driver helped her get them all inside and cautiously inquired if she would be ok there. She assured him she would be just fine, but she knew he doubted it and, frankly, so did she. He had glanced at her in his rearview

12

mirror occasionally on the drive out there and must have seen the waves of emotion surging through her. She went from feeling confident, intuitive, courageous and spontaneous one moment to terrified, impulsive, incompetent and irrational the next. She was known for her level-headed, dependable (and ultimately predictable) nature. Paul said he never wondered what she was thinking and her kids swore they knew what she would say before she said it – and they were usually right. At times Maggie felt proud of this – she was understood, knowable, transparent. At other times, she felt dull and unimaginative. Well – this decision would surely make jaws drop.

As the taxi crept up the driveway into her new life, fear and doubt were gaining the upper hand. She cleared her throat and was about to instruct the driver to take her back to the hotel when they again rounded the corner and there it was. The house. *Her* house. Imposing, dependable, welcoming, strong. She would craft a happy future here.

She paid the driver and shut and locked the front door. She toyed with the idea of phoning one of her children to let them know she changed her plans but decided against it. They could call her cell if they needed her. She wanted to savor her brave decision and her first night in her new home without the intrusion of their opinions.

Maggie picked up her groceries and headed in the direction of the kitchen. Dusty and in need of a thorough cleaning, to be sure, but what a glorious kitchen! Beautiful walnut cabinets adorned with furniture-maker details soared to the twelve-foot ceiling. A huge window over the old, French sink and a smaller window over an old-fashioned copper vegetable sink would make the room irresistibly cheerful in daytime. The appliances and fixtures were outdated and would need to be replaced, but it was still the most beautiful kitchen she had ever seen – much less owned. People will really have high expectations of a meal fixed here, she mused. I used to be such a good cook. I wonder if I can still muster up anything that does justice to this kitchen? I'll practice and get back on my game, she decided with a bit of her characteristic determination.

Maggie stashed her groceries and dug into the rotisserie chicken and coleslaw that she bought for her dinner. She began a systematic reconnaissance of the kitchen. To her delight, it was equipped with every specialty pot, pan, and utensil imaginable. I've been lusting after some of this stuff in catalogs for years, she thought. What great fun to cook in this kitchen.

Along one wall was an enormous antique hutch. Maggie found it contained five complete sets of china, including specialty pieces like eggcups, double-handled soup bowls, and tureens. She recognized Colombia Enamel by Wedgewood and Botanic Garden by Portmeiron, but had to check the bottom of a plate to see that she had place settings for twelve of Derby Panel by Royal Crown Derby and Lenox' lovely blue-rimmed favorite called Autumn. A set of cheerful yellow Fiestaware completed the collection. Good Lord – she felt faint. Maggie was a self-described china addict; now she had the collection to prove it. She vowed to use the good dishes every day.

Maggie made herself tea in a Wedgwood cup and wandered through the house to find a place to tuck herself away to enjoy it. The long day had taken its toll; she was exhausted. As she passed through the archway into the library she spotted an overstuffed chair in the moonlight by the French doors and knew she had found her spot. Maggie dragged the sheet off the chair with one hand while waving away a cloud of dust with the other and settled into its protective embrace.

The unblemished blanket of snow in the garden looked like frosting on a cake. Four inches already (at least) and it was still coming down hard. For the first time in months, everything around Maggie was quiet and still, and she felt peaceful. Thoughts of Paul were always crowding her, and they gradually settled on her now. Who was the man that she had been married to for over twenty-five years?

On the surface, Paul Martin was the charismatic President of Windsor College. Charming and handsome, with a killer smile. And laser focus. When he turned his attention on you, you felt like you were the most interesting and important person in the world. She had felt that way for years; had never doubted his integrity or fidelity. Mike and Susan, now both grown and out of the nest, adored their father. Paul's unexpected death at the age of sixty-two had unearthed a number of betrayals. Were there others as yet undiscovered? He evidently thought he had plenty of time to cover his tracks. Now Maggie was left to cope with it all.

The first shoe to drop was his embezzlement from the College. The Interim President discovered suspicious receipts in Paul's desk that he had been careless enough to leave sitting in a drawer. An audit was hastily done and the results discretely fed to her. Paul had been submitting fraudulent expenses as far back as they could trace, in excess of two million dollars. Where in the world had he been spending all of this money?

At first, Maggie wondered if Paul had a gambling problem. As she poured through the College's audit, however, it became very clear that the money was being spent in one location. Scottsdale, Arizona. And another fresh hell was born. She would never forget the day, last September, when she had summoned the courage to uncover the identity of the other woman.

Her short flight had been turbulent and, wedged into a middle seat between an overweight man with a dripping nose and a sprawling teenager, she was queasy by the time they landed. The taxi to the gate seemed interminable. She snatched her carry-on from the seatback in front of her the moment they came to a stop and shoved past the teen to get to the aisle, jostling the woman in the seat across the aisle as she attempted to stand up. "Getting a bit claustrophobic in there," she muttered in a half-hearted apology. The woman huffed and fixed Maggie with an icy stare. She didn't care what anyone thought; she needed to get off of this damn plane. The line in front of her inched along to the door. Why in the hell were people so slow and clumsy with their luggage? Why did they insist on stuffing bags into the overhead bins that they couldn't handle on their own? Just breathe deeply, she told herself.

The rental car was waiting for her. Thank goodness for the perks of being a frequent traveler. She settled into the seat and turned the air conditioner on full blast. Maggie fumbled in her purse for the report the private investigator had given her. She double-checked the address, but didn't need to; it was seared into her heart. Maggie punched it into the GPS system, adjusted her mirrors, and began her journey.

It was only ten o'clock in the morning, but near-record temperatures were predicted and heat waves shimmered off the highway. The GPS was reliable and she was close to "the street" in under thirty minutes. Maggie decided she needed something to drink and turned into a convenience store to get a giant diet cola and a bottle of cold water. No one was behind her in line and she took her time in fishing out the correct change. Now that she was here, she wasn't so sure she wanted to pick at this scab. She lingered over the rack of tabloid magazines by the door. What was the matter with her? She was just going to drive by a house. She probably wouldn't even see "her." She had come all of this way – she needed to hitch up her britches and do this thing.

Maggie coiled herself into the now oven-like car and burned her hands as she grasped the steering wheel. She took a long pull on her diet cola and set off once more. She drove slowly as the ascending street numbers indicated she was getting close. Undeniably a swanky neighborhood, she brooded. Nicer than ours. Spacious, new stucco homes with red-tile roofs and soaring arches. Intricate iron gates and ornate light fixtures. Manicured lawns tended by efficient landscapers. No signs of life on this oppressive day. Everyone was safely tucked away.

And there it was. Bigger than the rest – or was she imaging that? It was unquestionably the nicest house on the street and bile rose in Maggie's throat. If you had lined up photos of all of the houses and asked her which one Paul would have selected, Maggie knew it would have been this house. More grand than their home in California. Maggie drifted across the centerline and caught herself before she hit the other curb. Thank God she was the only car on the street. She needed to get hold of herself; she didn't want to get into an accident right outside the other woman's house. How cliché would that be? She was acting like a stalker, for goodness sake. No one could ever know she had done this.

She turned around in a driveway five houses down and drove past to view it from the other direction. Shit – it looked even better. That bastard. She tightened her grip on the steering wheel and turned the car around again, trying to find a shady spot along the curb where she could discretely watch the house. A couple of palm trees provided the only shade available and she pulled to the curb. The air conditioning was no match for the midday sun and she felt like the ants under the magnifying glass that her brother fried on the sidewalk when they were kids. Why in the world had

Paul done this? Why hadn't they just divorced? Was he that concerned about the effect it would have on his career? Divorce wasn't a stigma anymore. And he evidently had plenty of money so splitting what they had in California wouldn't have posed a problem. Surely he knew that she would never have gone digging for more. Or was he addicted to the thrill of living a secret life? She instinctively knew she had hit the mark dead center. Her soda was long gone and she was taking the last swig of water, chiding herself that it was demeaning to be sweltering in a rental car outside of the other woman's house, when *she* appeared.

Maggie crouched over the dashboard, the air conditioning blasting her hair out of her face, and focused on the other woman like a laser. Tall, thin, and pretty – with shoulder-length blonde hair and long, tanned legs – she was laughing with two school-aged children as she herded them into her Escalade. She pulled out of the driveway and glanced in Maggie's direction as she turned to say something to the children in the back seat.

Maggie clutched the steering wheel as nausea overwhelmed her. She tried unsuccessfully to choke it back and grabbed frantically for the empty soda cup and heaved violently. Sweating profusely, she fumbled in her purse for some tissues and a breath mint. The tears she had been holding back for months now broke free. This had been a stupid, crazy thing to do. Why had she expected it to turn out differently? She was a mess. Vomit on her cuff and in her hair. The last thing she wanted to do was spend the day here and get back on a plane later. To hell with the one-way drop-off charge for the rental car. It was only a six-hour drive. She'd be in her driveway about the same time as her scheduled flight was supposed to arrive. And she wouldn't have to see anyone or talk to anyone along the way. She swung the car around and set her course for home.

The minute she uncovered the Scottsdale connection, Maggie knew in her gut what she would find. Paul supported a second family there. The investigator found that the children weren't Paul's, thank God. But they had a long-standing relationship and by the looks of the financial records, he had been supporting her handsomely. The most difficult part of Maggie's situation was bearing this knowledge alone; she dared not confide in anyone she knew.

Paul had been acting strangely since he took the post at Windsor College eight years ago. She had done her best to contrive an innocent explanation and rationalize Paul's odd behaviors. But everything now made sense; the weekends away, when he was ostensibly too tied up in strategic-planning sessions to call home; his new, trendy wardrobe and haircut; and his younger, more "hip" vocabulary. When Susan remarked on them, Paul laughed and passed them off as his way of relating to the student body.

He had also become increasingly critical of her blossoming consulting business as a forensic accountant. At first, she believed he was genuinely concerned she was taking on too much and spreading herself too thin. He was emphatic that he needed her by his side for the numerous social engagements required by his position. Somewhere along the way she realized that he resented her success and her growing independence from him. Paul loved to tell his amusing little story about meeting a shy, studious, plain girl in college and turning her into the beautiful, polished, accomplished woman she was now; that their love story was a modern-day *My Fair Lady*. Ugh!! She may not have been a sophisticate, but she hadn't been a country bumpkin, either. Even Eliza Doolittle outgrew the tutelage of Professor Higgins.

The turning point in their relationship was that horrible fight about the black-tie fundraiser he wanted to chair. He would turn up at the event in his tuxedo and make a nice podium speech, and she would work tirelessly on it for almost a year. She had begged him not to volunteer, that she simply didn't have the time, that just this once she needed to focus on herself first. She was about to land a lucrative expert witness engagement she had worked so hard to get. It was a fascinating case and would demand all of her time. And would undoubtedly lead to more such work. She simply could not turn it down.

Paul had railed that he couldn't turn it down, either. He started on his usual refrain of "whose job pays more of the bills around here" when Maggie quietly pointed out that her income had exceeded his for several years. For the first time in their more than twenty years of marriage, Maggie had put her foot down and told Paul "No". Paul had exploded and they had gone to bed angry.

This time, however, Maggie didn't give in and apologize just to keep the peace.

They didn't speak for a week. When they tentatively resumed communication, Paul was derisive and demeaning, constantly criticizing Maggie in matters both large and small. His opinion of her appearance, her job and her social skills didn't matter much to Maggie anymore. Maggie's friend Helen summed it up nicely; Paul had lost control of Maggie and he didn't like it. She had half-heartedly defended Paul, saying he was a leader and not a control freak, but she knew Helen was right.

Her lawyer negotiated a settlement of the College's claim against Paul's estate in exchange for his million-dollar life insurance policy. The Board of Regents hadn't been anxious to have their lax oversight of the College's finances exposed, and Maggie didn't want Mike and Susan hurt by a public discrediting of Paul's memory. She needed to get to the bottom of the mystery that was Paul Martin before she brought Mike and Susan into this nightmare. Maggie hired a private investigator that quickly uncovered the truth.

Revisiting these horribly hurtful revelations – so frustrating because Paul was not there to question, cross-examine, rage at – was like watching a tornado relentlessly obliterate her lovingly crafted life. The outcome – the pain and loss and desolation – were constant companions. But tonight, sunk into this massive chair within the perfect stillness, Maggie removed herself from the starring role and felt like she was watching someone else's tragedy. She let her mind go blank and watched the snow slanting down across the tree outside her window. And she surrendered to a deep and dreamless sleep.

Having his office above his liquor store had its advantages; Chuck Delgado was well into the bottle of Jameson he grabbed from behind the counter as he waited for Frank Haynes to arrive on this Godforsaken night. Shortly after two in the morning, Haynes tapped quietly on the back door, below. Delgado checked the security camera and buzzed him up. Haynes firmly climbed the steps into Delgado's lair.

19

He was slumped in his chair just outside the pool of light supplied by the green-shaded lamp on his desk. Haynes scanned the room, allowing his eyes to adjust to the dimness. The rest of the room was in shadow and Haynes was glad of it. He didn't care to be accosted by Delgado's collection of crude, pornographic trinkets and toys.

Delgado shoved the open bottle and a highball glass in his direction. Haynes firmly declined. He didn't need to get light-headed now and God knows when that glass had last been washed. He cast a dubious glance at the two chairs across the desk from Delgado and moved a stack of newspapers and a hamburger wrapper onto the floor. At least he's patronizing one of my restaurants, he thought.

They regarded each other intently. Haynes remained silent.

Delgado nursed his drink and Haynes sat, brooding and impassive. Delgado finally sucked in a deep breath and began. "OK, Frank, here's the thing. We ran into an unexpected situation."

Haynes raised an eyebrow.

"Not with anything here. Operations in Westbury are fine. In Florida. It's hard to keep your finger on things from a distance. I sent Wheeler down to check on things, but the bastard spent all his time with the whores in the condos. I understand a guy's gotta have fun, but he didn't do jack shit down there. Bastard lied to me when he got back. If this all goes down, that dumb fuck deserves to take the fall." Delgado gave a satisfied nod and sank back into his chair.

Haynes leaned rigidly forward, resting his elbows on his knees, and locked Delgado with his glare. He waited until Delgado, hand shaking, set his drink down.

"We aren't going to let this 'all go down', Charles, now are we? We aren't going to let that happen. We had plenty of cushion built in to survive even the recession. If you hadn't dipped your hand in the till, we wouldn't be having this unfortunate conversation."

"Jesus, Frank. I had stuff to take care of. Those cops down there are expensive and…"

He stopped in mid-sentence as Haynes slammed a fist on the desk and roared, "Silence! I don't give a fuck what situation you got your sorry ass into. You know that you were not to bring your other sordid business interests into our arrangement. Those condos were supposed to be legitimate investments, not whore houses or meth labs or whatever other Godforsaken activities you've got going in them."

Delgado held up a hand in a gesture of surrender. "You're right, Frank, I know you are. But shit happens. I'll get this figured out. I may have buyers for a couple of the condos. And I'm expecting money from another associate next week. Enough to fund the shortfall in the next pension payments. Don't go gettin' yourself into an uproar. We'll get things straightened out. I'm on it," he slurred.

"You've got ten days to get this handled," Haynes growled. "I'm going to watch your every move from here on in. You won't want to disappoint me." His tone sent a wave of fear and dread through Delgado.

Haynes rose slowly, turned on his heel and walked purposely down the stairs, allowing the echo of his steps to recede before he opened the back door and was swallowed by the night.

"Jesus," Delgado muttered when he could no longer hear Haynes' car retreating. "That guy is one scary mother-fucker." He reached for the bottle and didn't bother with a glass.

Chapter 2

An insistent crying woke Maggie. She was shocked to see it was fully light out. She checked her watch and was amazed to see it was almost nine o'clock. She hadn't slept this late in months. She hoisted herself out of the chair and turned toward the French doors. On the other side, in the shelter of a tree, was a snow-covered dog, whimpering miserably. You poor thing, Maggie thought. She wrangled with the lock and opened the door. The dog raced into the house like it had been shot from a gun, skidded to a halt in the middle of the library and vigorously shook itself, sending snow around the room like shrapnel.

Maggie dropped to one knee, held out a hand, and coaxed the animal to her. "Well, who are you?" Maggie spoke softly to the dog. "No collar, no tags. Do you belong to somebody?" The small female terrier mix, white with brown markings, sidled over to her and firmly planted her muzzle in Maggie's lap. "You are a soppy mess," she said. "Let's get you dried off. Are you hungry?"

Maggie scavenged a towel from the closet off of the laundry room. "OK – let's get you fed. I don't have any dog food and we are snowed in at the moment, so you're going to get people food. Don't get used to it." As the dog practically inhaled the remainder of last night's chicken, Maggie decided that unless she belonged to someone, she was going to keep her. Paul always threw cold water on Maggie's desire to have a dog – they traveled too much, worked too many hours, it wouldn't be fair to the animal, on and on. In truth, he wasn't a dog person. And she always suspected that she was. Maggie now had a new companion for her new life. She named her Eve.

Maggie dusted off the coffee maker and filled a solid stoneware mug with a large cup of strong black coffee. She summoned Eve and they headed upstairs to choose the bedroom and bathroom that she would settle into.

After narrowing her favorites down to the two bedrooms at either end of the house, she selected the large room that ran the width of the house along the east side, with shuttered windows on three sides, a cozy fireplace, and a generous marble bath. The morning sun sought every corner and painted the space into an Impressionistic prettiness. What a pleasure to make a decision based solely on what I want, without considering anybody else, she realized. Removing the sheets from the furniture and cleaning it would have to wait. Right now she wanted to grab a quick shower and change out of the clothes she had slept in. The hot water was plentiful. She stood in the steamy shower and allowed the water to wash away the recent gloom that pervaded her. She was pulling on an old pair of jeans and a sweater when she heard the snowplow laboring up the drive. She grabbed her shoes and raced down the stairs, with Eve keeping pace.

Maggie threw on her coat, wound her scarf around her neck and stepped out the front door as the plow finished clearing the turn-around in front of the house. The driver didn't see her signaling him to stop and proceeded back down the driveway. She was looking forlornly in the direction of the retreating plow when a neat old pickup truck slowly made its way up the drive. Maggie recognized the driver. Sam had come to check on her. She smiled and waved as he pulled up.

"How'd you get along last night?" he called as he stepped out of his truck. By his tone, she knew he had been worried about her. "Did the furnace hold up?"

She assured him that all had been just fine, with lots of warm air and hot water. "I've already had a visitor this morning. Come inside and meet Eve" she said, and told him about waking up to find her outside, in the snow.

"Well…how 'bout that. It's a wonder she survived," he noted as he scratched her behind the ears. "I've never seen her before. I don't think she belongs to anyone around here."

"Good, because I'd like to keep her. Will you watch for any Lost Dog notices? I'll contact a local vet and check online to see if any dogs have been reported missing, and if not, she's my new roommate."

"This place is seeing more life than it has in years," Sam declared. "Here's some banana bread, yogurt and fruit from my wife for you. We don't want to impose, but we'd like you to join us for dinner tonight. She says you have a lot of cleaning to do in your kitchen before you can use it."

Maggie acknowledged that his wife was right about that. "This is all very kind of you," she said, gesturing to the goodies she was holding. "But you don't need to have me over for dinner. I've got groceries."

"Joan would really like to meet you. Once word gets out about you staying on at Rosemont, you'll be the talk of the town. And we'll be able to say that we know you," he said with a twinkle in his eye.

Maggie laughed. "I've never been 'the talk of the town' before. I assure you, I'm very boring. My time in the limelight will pass quickly. But I'd like the opportunity to get to know you both and my new hometown better. So thank you. I'd love to come to dinner."

"Wonderful" he exclaimed. "I'll pick you up at four o'clock, dinner is at five – if that's ok. We like to eat supper early on Sunday night." He turned to go, stopped, and looked back at her. "I have a fairly open week next week, so if you need any help or need a ride anywhere, just let me know." With that he stepped outside and headed back to his truck.

"OK, Eve" Maggie said. "My first social engagement is on the books. What shall we do until then?

Maggie took Joan's care package to her new bedroom, broke off a generous piece of the fragrant bread and shared it with Eve. Eve selected a spot in the sun slanting onto the fireplace rug, circled three times, and settled in for a morning nap.

Maggie set to work with a vengeance uncovering the furniture and dusting, scrubbing and vacuuming every surface. She lost herself in the task at hand – restoring order to her new environment was cathartic. If her emotional life was in turmoil, at least her bedroom was clean. And for now, that was enough.

It was three-thirty when she finished – just enough time to dig out something a bit more presentable to wear to dinner and to dash off a quick text to Susan and Mike that she was fine, the house was great, and she would call them later that night.

Sam arrived promptly at four and insisted that the invitation included Eve. Delighted, Eve leapt onto Maggie's lap and they set off through the bright, clear afternoon. The snow had stopped and the landscape was iridescent.

The Torres' lived on the other side of the Town Square. Westbury was the county seat and home to some forty-thousand residents. The Square was dominated by the County Courthouse, an imposing building of indigenous limestone in the grand style popular in the late 1800s, with sixty-foot columns flanking the entries at both the north and south sides and ringed with carved figures along the top. The limestone was tarnished with soot and the ravages of age, but the Courthouse was still beautiful. It was surrounded on all four sides by a generous lawn and a row of stately oak trees. An old-fashioned bandstand stood in one corner of the lawn.

"How charming," Maggie commented. "Does that bandstand actually get used, or is it just for show?"

"We use it," Sam told her with pride. "April through December. We have band concerts, choral groups, Wednesday-night cloggers. You name it." He glanced at Maggie. She smiled in encouragement and raised an eyebrow. Sam warmed to his topic. "If you don't know, cloggers are sort of like country-western tap dancers. If you've never seen clogging, you'll be amazed. You might want to try it. It's a lot of fun. And they hold big country-western dances on the Square. Joan and I attend those. They have craft fairs three or four times a year. And the Courthouse is decorated with more holiday lights than any other building in the state. We have a big lighting ceremony every year on December first."

"Sounds lovely. Homey and old-timey and congenial. Very neighborly. I've always lived in a big city and we just didn't do that. Something to look forward to."

She turned her attention back to the area around the Square. Rows of intricate, architecturally-interesting brick buildings that originally must have housed wealthy residents and more recently shops and businesses surrounded the Square. Almost half of them were boarded and empty, with "Available" signs posted above the entrances.

"Looks like the recession's hit Westbury like it's hit everywhere else," Maggie observed.

"That and more," Sam answered cryptically as they pulled into his driveway.

Joan Torres flung the front door open in welcome before Maggie could get out of the truck. If she was surprised to see Eve, Joan didn't let on. She welcomed Maggie with a warm handshake and gave Eve a good rub. Maggie presented Joan with a bottle of wine she had uncovered in her pantry and followed her into the living room. "Something smells absolutely delicious!" Maggie exclaimed. "And that banana bread was fabulous. You're a lifesaver."

Maggie took a seat by the fireplace as Sam uncorked the wine and handed each of them a glass. "Sam tells me that you're going to keep Rosemont. We'll all be so happy to see that house occupied again. Will you live here full time?" Joan asked. She was curious about this sophisticated widow who would now be part of their community.

"Yes. I'll get myself set up here and go back home long enough to pack and put my house on the market. My kids are grown and I have my own consulting business. I'm a forensic accountant. My clients are all over North America and I do most of my work over the phone and internet." Maybe it was the wine, on top of the sheer fatigue of the past months, coupled with the soothing warmth of the fire; Maggie found herself pouring out her hurt and uncertainty. "Frankly, this has been a snap decision on my part. I came here out of curiosity to see the place. I never knew that Paul had inherited Rosemont. I intended to sell it. But when the front door closed behind me, I knew I was home. And that I need a fresh start. In this spot." She glanced at their anxious faces and saw that they didn't know exactly how to respond. "Paul was so prominent in our community that I can't go anywhere without being reminded of him" she said, and her voice choked with emotion. "I've found out things about him since he died that have been very hurtful." She looked away from them now. "I

26

can't discuss this with anyone back home. My kids adore their father and if even half of it gets out, his reputation will be ruined. I can't bear thinking about what that would do to my kids." Maggie took a raged breath and turned back to her hosts. "I'm so sorry. I shouldn't have burdened you with my worries. This isn't what you bargained for when you invited me to dinner. Please, just forget I said anything," she implored.

Joan leaned over and squeezed her hand. "We're not gossips. We won't repeat anything you've told us. I know what it's like to need a friend you can count on," she said. "We've only just met, but I hope you consider us such friends."

Maggie looked into the earnest eyes of this kindly couple, so unlike the flashy and urbane people she and Paul considered friends, and knew that they were genuine and trustworthy. How long had it been since she had felt so comfortable – so unguarded – with supposed friends? Maggie squeezed Joan's hand in return. "I guess I felt that the minute I met you." She drew a deep breath and relaxed into her chair. "So, do you know the history of Rosemont?"

"Oh, heavens yes," Joan replied. "Everybody around here knows about Rosemont. It was built in 1893 by Silas Martin. He made his fortune from the local sawmill, which was turned into a hotel and restaurant in the late 1920's. It's still there. And he later invested in property all over town. Was instrumental in raising funds to build our Courthouse. He was three times a widower and had five children – all boys. Two died in childhood and one was killed in World War I. Legend has it that Silas was unbearably autocratic in his later years and drove away his son Joseph, who became a successful attorney in Cleveland and had one son. The other son, Hector, remained in Westbury and expanded his father's business interests and fortune. He never married. Hector inherited the property when Silas died in 1937 and left it to his brother Joseph's grandson when Hector died in 2000 at the age of one hundred and six. Your husband was Joseph's grandson, I believe?"

"Yes," Maggie replied. "Paul's father died the year before we got married and his mother died when he was in kindergarten. He told me he had no living relatives. Paul never once mentioned Westbury or Rosemont. Not even when he inherited it." Maggie saw shock register on Joan's face. She continued, "Do you know if Paul ever spent time here growing up? Was he close to Hector?" She inhaled deeply and her voice trembled, "Has Paul spent any time here since he became the owner?"

Sam leaned over and looked her squarely in the eyes. "I don't think Paul spent any time here when he was growing up. I met him once, briefly, three or four years ago when he came to town and hired me to make repairs at Rosemont. He told me he wanted to fix the place up as a surprise for his family." He paused to let this sink in. "He put me on retainer to keep the place in good repair, and he hired a crew to maintain the grounds. We had very little contact. He always paid me on time. We were sorry to hear about his death. And your loss," he concluded gently.

Maggie let out a long, slow breath. "Thank you for this. I've been so curious about Paul's connection to Westbury and Rosemont, but didn't know anyone to ask." She was tremendously relieved that Paul had not been bringing the other woman and her children here. Maybe Paul had meant it to be a surprise for her and the kids all along? This thought was vaguely comforting. Joan broke Maggie's reverie by announcing that dinner was ready.

Over a generous helping of the best pot roast Maggie had had in years, she learned that Sam was a custodian at the local elementary school and Joan was a dispatcher for the Westbury Police Department. They were both born there and had been high school sweethearts. They had three grown children, seven grandchildren, and were active members of the Methodist Church. Their hobby was travel and they took one big trip each summer. They funded their travels by taking on extra jobs. Sam did handyman work after school each afternoon and on Saturdays and Joan took in sewing and alterations.

"So where are you headed on your next trip?" Maggie asked, and instantly regretted it. Joan began twisting her napkin and the couple exchanged a wary glance.

Sam sighed, "We don't have anything planned at the moment. We hoped to go to Italy this summer, but we're holding off. Westbury is in terrible financial shape. We both have over thirty years of seniority and aren't worried about being laid off, but we've had unpaid furlough days and there is talk that the Town's pension fund wasn't properly invested and is broke."

28

Joan brought one hand to her chest and leaned forward. "We've worked long and hard all our lives, been model employees. And now we don't know if our retirement is secure or not. We're in our early sixties. We can't replace all of that money now. We've always lived within our budget, which wasn't always easy. Put our kids through college. We thought that our retirement would be the time for us to do what we wanted."

Maggie was shocked. "What do you mean "broke"?" she asked. "Aren't the Town's financials audited each year? How could that even be possible?" And then she thought about Paul's financial misdeeds – Paul who was widely thought to be above reproach by everyone – and realized that this terrible suspicion might be true.

"William Wheeler has been our Mayor for thirteen years, and his dad was Mayor before him. Things ran pretty well for a long time. This is fertile land and our farm families have done well. We were home to several large manufacturing plants. When the manufacturing jobs went to China and the factories wound down, they brought in a couple of high-end golf courses and tourism took over where the factories left off. But with this recession, tourism is way down. The shops that were supported by our visitors are struggling and no one is buying second homes on the golf courses."

Sam continued, "Wheeler's cronies make up our Town Council. Or they did until last year when we elected our first independent Councilperson, Tonya Holmes. She discovered the shortage in the pension account. This is all just starting to come to light. We don't know what's true or where to turn. I don't trust Wheeler and his bunch, that's for sure. Tonya is having a town hall meeting Wednesday night at the Library to tell everyone what she's found out so far. We'll be in the front row," he said vehemently.

"Is she working with anyone on this? You may want to get a forensic accountant involved. As I said, that's my specialty. I can recommend someone if you'd like. Here's my card," Maggie said, fishing one out of her purse. "The number is my cell. You can tell Tonya to call me, if she'd like. I'd be happy to talk with her. I'm so sorry – this is just terrible. I hope you find it's not as bad as you think."

Sam took the card. "We do, too. Thank you. Enough of this -- what do you plan to do tomorrow?"

"I'll rent a car. I want to get Eve to the vet to see if she has a microchip. I'm getting very attached to her. If she has an owner, I need to return her as soon as possible." Maggie sighed. "And I'll tell the realtor I'm not selling. Then I should get the house in shape to move into. I haven't even uncovered all of the furniture or figured out what repairs are needed or changes I'd like to make." Maggie turned to face Sam. "Would you have time to help me assess the house and to make the necessary repairs?"

"Absolutely. I'm not the fastest handyman around, but I'm also not the most expensive and I don't believe anyone does better work than I do. I work alone, at my own pace. I've found that a lot of mistakes can be avoided if you think things through first. If I need help, I can call on another maintenance man from the school. He takes on extra jobs, too. We've worked together for over thirty years, so we know each other's ways and habits, strengths and weaknesses. We make a good team. And I'll always get you the best materials at the lowest price. I'll tell you where to cut corners, and when you can't. If you don't like something I've done, I'll redo it until you're happy. As simple as that."

"Sounds perfect. When can you start?"

Maggie was bone tired when she turned back the sheets and climbed into the new, unfamiliar bed. Eve leapt up easily, circled around, and settled at Maggie's feet. She mentally replayed her conversations with Mike and Susan a few hours earlier. She hoped she had done the right thing by remaining silent about her decision to uproot her life and move to Westbury. Maggie wasn't ready to get into a big discussion about it yet.

Maybe they were just too busy with their own lives -- Mike with getting the twins to bed and Susan with preparing for a hearing in one of her cases – but they didn't seem overly interested in what had been going on in her world. They were satisfied with her quick report about the house and the weather, and accepted without question her news that it would take a bit longer for her to finish her business in Westbury. She nestled into the crisp sheets and was caressed by sleep as Eve faintly snored at her feet.

Chapter 3

Maggie woke early the next morning, rested and ready to launch into her new life. First priorities were to pick up a rental car and take Eve to the vet for a good once over. She also needed dog food and cleaning supplies. She arranged to get the car at the hotel on the Square right after lunch and made an appointment with the nearest vet, John Allen, DVM. It was going to be another cold, sunny day and she and Eve could walk through the Square to his office for their mid-morning appointment.

Maggie uncovered the downstairs furniture before they set out for Eve's appointment. Rosemont was filled with lovely antiques. Some of the upholstery had seen better days, but it all looked serviceable. Cleaning this place, however, was going to be a huge task.

Maggie fashioned a makeshift collar and leash out of twine that she found in a kitchen drawer, and she and Eve set out into the bright morning. Eve was well-mannered on the leash and Maggie's heart sank as she worried that Eve might have an owner who would be looking for her. She pushed the thought from her mind as they walked past the storefronts lining the Square.

The window of Laura's Bakery stopped them both in their tracks. A tiered stand showcased elaborately-iced cakes flanked by pies sporting flaky, golden crusts. The wonderful aroma of baking bread rolled out into the street. A water dish by the entrance invited Eve to take a drink. A sign in the window announced the town hall meeting at the Library on Wednesday night.

As Eve lapped up a long drink, the pretty young woman placing a tray of cupcakes in a case looked up and smiled. Maggie nodded and smiled in return and the tall, dark-haired woman quickly came to the door and beckoned them both in. "We don't discriminate against dogs here," Laura Fitzpatrick assured them. "She can come in. I don't believe we've met. Are you visiting Westbury?" Laura asked.

"No. I'm in the process of moving here." Maggie held out her hand to Laura as they shook and introduced themselves. "I inherited Rosemont and arrived here two days ago. I'm going to make Westbury my home."

"Terrific – how exciting! I'm fairly new here myself. I moved to Westbury three years ago when Pete and I got married. Pete runs the bistro next door. Have you seen it yet? We're connected right through that doorway past the case. You can get a pastry here and take it next door to eat it with a cup of the best coffee in town. He has live music on Friday and Saturday nights. If you don't want rowdy dance music, you can go to Pete's for really good jazz and folk music from local artists. And you can get free wifi."

Maggie smiled at the obvious pride that this confident young woman – Susan's age? – displayed in her business. "You'll see a lot of me, then," she told Laura. "I'm a consultant and am online all day long. I need to get internet service set up at Rosemont, but I like to get out of the house to work, too. So I'll be back. And I'll be hungry," she assured Laura.

"And who is this?" Laura asked, pointing to Eve.

"I've named her Eve," Maggie said and launched into the tale of their meeting. "We're headed to Dr. Allen's right now to get her checked out. I'm pretty attached to her already. I hope she doesn't have an owner." Maggie sighed.

"She's a sweet thing, isn't she," Laura observed. "I haven't seen her around, and we get a lot of dogs in here," she said, gesturing to the water bowl. "I hope you can keep her. And that the two of you become regulars." She reached into a jar under the counter and came out with a dog biscuit for Eve. "When you come back, pick a cupcake for yourself, my treat."

Maggie reluctantly left the warmth of the shop for the chilly street. She glanced at her watch and realized that they would have to hustle to make their appointment on time. Exploring any of the other shops would have to wait.

They set off at a trot and Maggie reached for the door of the Westbury Animal Hospital as it was being opened by a tall man in a cashmere sport coat wielding a large animal carrier. Maggie stepped back to allow him to pass with his awkward load, but he insisted that she take the right of way as he held the door. He set his carrier on the floor and got down on one knee to greet Eve. He knows her, Maggie realized as her heart plummeted to her shoes. She paused to collect herself while the man accepted Eve's effusive greeting. Darn it, she thought, I'm going to have to give her up. Just when I thought things were changing for me. He looks nice and Eve seems to like him, but I wanted her for me. Maggie knew she was being childish, but frankly didn't care. Wasn't it high time things went her way?

The man turned to Maggie as he stood up. "This dog escaped from the Forever Friends shelter. We've been worried sick about her, what with the storm that moved in. I'm so glad she's well and that you found her," he said as he reached for the leash.

Maggie took a step back and kept a firm hold on the leash. "So she's not your dog? She's up for adoption?" she asked in a voice that radiated relief and hope. Before he could answer, she extended her hand. "I'm Maggie Martin."

"Frank Haynes," he answered as he shook her hand. "Yes, she is. Or she will be. We need to have her checked out by the vet here before we put her up for adoption."

"I was bringing her in to do just that," Maggie replied. "Why don't you let me take care of that for you. If she gets the go ahead from the vet, I'd like to adopt her. Can we arrange that? I'll pay whatever fee you charge."

Haynes regarded her thoughtfully. Maggie Martin. He hadn't heard of her before. Hadn't seen her around. Attractive, probably in her 50's, articulate and self-assured. Expensively dressed. Probably some self-important professional woman. God – the place was getting overrun by them. Like that insufferable Tonya Holmes on the Council. He snapped his attention back to the woman who was eyeing him curiously, waiting for his reply.

"Yes. I'm sure that would be fine." He reached into the breast pocket of his jacket and produced a business card for Forever Friends. "Just call the shelter and they can take care of the paperwork. I'll let them know we've agreed to this arrangement."

34

"Thank you so much," Maggie gushed and shook his hand again warmly. He fought the urge to recoil. "I'm thrilled to have her. We're starting a new life together."

At this odd remark, something clicked in Haynes' computer-like memory. He brought his left hand to grasp their joined hands. "Martin, did you say? Are you related to the late Paul Martin?"

The mention of Paul's name still sent an unpleasant shiver through Maggie. She tried to withdraw her hand but he was holding her captive. "Yes. He was my husband. Did you know Paul?"

"My condolences, Mrs. Martin. No. I never met him. I heard you were coming to town to list Rosemont for sale," he probed, wondering why in the world she would be adopting a dog here to take home to California. Haynes had done his homework. He had admired Rosemont for as long as he could remember. Had walked by it and daydreamed about it as a kid from the wrong side of the tracks and had lusted after it as a wealthy self-made businessman. He was determined to buy it and knew that the owner was a widow who lived in California. With the depressed state of the luxury real estate market, he planned to let it sit on the market for six months and pick it up with a low-ball offer when the stress of maintaining an aging property became too much for the suffering widow. He would let the realtor know he was interested and not to accept any offers without checking with him first. In the unlikely event someone came along to buy the place, he could always come in with a strong cash offer. But no point in overpaying if he didn't have to.

She was once more regarding him curiously. "Rumors do fly in a small town, don't they?" she commented as she forcefully extricated her hand from his grasp. "I've decided not to sell Rosemont. I'm going to keep it and move here instead. That's why I've adopted Eve."

Haynes felt like she had slapped him across the face with the back of her hand. How dare she? Dammit. He wanted that house! If he had Rosemont, everyone in this stinking town would know that he had made it. No one would look down their nose at his lack of a fancy education or his fast-food franchises, whose menus they criticized but whose convenience they loved. He was tired of feeling like everyone branded him as blue-collar, even though his suits cost thousands of dollars, he donated generously to every sports team and charity, and held a spot on that group of idiots they called a Town Council. Owning Rosemont would bring it all together for him. Before long, people would forget that he hadn't lived there all along. Haynes realized that he had stopped listening to her. She was rambling on about some stupid job of hers – about how she could work at home – could work anywhere in the country. And a flash of brilliance hit him. Maybe he could move into Rosemont without buying it. He gave this Maggie Martin another going over. She would be considered attractive. Self-sufficient, probably. Maybe it was time for him to reconsider his aversion to remarrying? He involuntarily shuddered at the thought. He'd give it some time. She might grow tired of the house or this town and run back to southern California with her tail between her legs. He might be able to pick up Rosemont even cheaper as a result. The thought positively cheered him.

Haynes forced a smile onto his lips that wasn't mirrored in the harsh lines around his eyes. "Welcome to Westbury, then. Be sure to stop by the shelter to complete the paperwork for Eve." Before Maggie could respond, the technician signaled that it was time for Eve's appointment. Haynes turned on his heel and strode out the door.

Maggie's first impression of Dr. John Allen, DVM, was of a man with a gentle nature and deep, abiding kindness. He was of medium height, with a strong frame that gave him a substantial appearance. Dark hair, graying at the temples, and clear blue eyes. In his mid-fifties? She instantly liked him.

"How can I help you?" John asked after introducing himself.

Maggie told him she was in the process of moving to Westbury and once again repeated her tale of how she first met Eve. "I've been worried that she has an owner, but I ran into a man on the way in here that said she escaped from a rescue shelter and if she checks out by you, I can adopt her."

"Ah, yes. That would be Frank Haynes. He's the driving force behind the shelter. Ok – let's get her on the exam table and take a look. She doesn't seem the worse for wear for spending the night out in the storm."

Maggie held the squirming dog while the vet took her vital signs and began his exam. "Has she been eating and drinking?"

"Yes – just fine. And she's house-broken. How old do you think she is? Is she full grown?"

Dr. Allen examined her white, smooth teeth. "She's a young dog – full grown – but probably only a year or eighteen months old. Still a lot of puppy left in her. She's tolerating all of this very well. You'll want to get her spayed as soon as you can. She'll live longer and be healthier if you do. You're not going to breed her?"

"Absolutely not. I'll be returning to California next week. Can I have that done while I'm gone? I'll be away for about ten days. Is that too long to leave her here? Do you do boarding?"

"We do. That should work just fine."

Maggie took Eve in her arms and nuzzled her neck. John thought to himself that they would bring each other a great deal of happiness, as pets often did to lonely people. Including himself.

"I've never owned a dog before. I don't know what to do," she admitted frankly. "Can you give me a crash course on what I need to know? Do you have a pamphlet or something?" she asked, casting her eyes around the exam room.

What a sweet, open spirit, he thought to himself. Who is this gorgeous woman that just stepped into my world?

He laughed. "It's not complicated. Yearly shots, dog food twice a day. No people food or scraps" he warned sternly, figuring her to be a light touch to a begging animal. "Grooming and walks, and you've pretty much got it covered. You'll be a pro in no time," he assured her. "Can you leave her with me for the day? We'll check her over completely, give her shots and a bath. I'll send you home with a sample of dog food and you can get more if she likes it. You can pick her up between four and five."

Maggie heaved a sigh of relief. "Perfect. And can you put a microchip in her for me? We've both just moved into Rosemont," she stated, thinking again that she really *was* going to do this – just pull up stakes and relocate her life to Westbury.

Maggie left Eve in the capable custody of the Westbury Animal Hospital and stepped out into the brisk late morning. She decided to pick up a sandwich at Pete's on the way home. Laura greeted her like an old friend and, already, she was beginning to feel like she was a part of this place. As she wound up the long driveway to Rosemont, she started a mental list of the many tasks ahead of her. She dreaded telling the realtor, who had been delighted at the prospect of listing Rosemont, that she wouldn't be selling after all. She toyed with the idea of calling him, but decided that would be cowardly and he deserved to be told face to face. Maggie wanted to get off on the right foot in Westbury, and realtors know everybody in a small town. She'd get it over with after lunch.

The car was ready as promised and, after providing vague answers to a flurry of nosey questions from the rental agency clerk, she plucked Tim Knudsen's card from her wallet, entered his address in the car's GPS and set off. She arrived fifteen minutes early, but Tim was waiting for her and ushered her into his office.

Maggie quickly got to the point. "I'm terribly sorry to have wasted your time, but I've decided to keep Rosemont. I'm going to live there full time."

Tim was surprised, but if he was disappointed, he didn't let on. "Rosemont is one of the most distinct properties in this area. I've admired it since I was a little boy. The best outcome is for it to remain the private home of someone who appreciates it. There's been speculation over the years that it would become an assisted-living facility or bed and breakfast. I wouldn't want either of those."

Maggie settled into her chair, relieved at his good-natured loss of a lucrative listing and that he wasn't trying to change her mind by bringing up all of the obvious challenges to maintaining the historic home and spacious grounds.

"I never met your late husband. My condolences on his death. Will you be working here in Westbury?" Tim was obviously interested in this development. Like all realtors, he was a repository of the history and news of his area. He sensed that he had a scoop in the making.

"I'm a consultant. My clients are all over the country and I work from home," she said. "I'm going to spend the next week trying to get Rosemont cleaned up. Then I'll go back to California to pack up my house and put it on the market."

Tim thoughtfully considered this information and offered to help her with referrals to any service she needed. "Surely you're not going to clean that entire house by yourself? Would you like me to arrange housekeepers to come out? Even with an experienced crew, it will take the best part of a week to clean that place. And the finest handyman around is Sam Torres," he opined.

Maggie smiled at the mention of Sam's name. She told him about meeting Sam and having Sunday supper at the Torres home.

"That sounds just like them. People around here are decent and generous and kind. You'll like it here," Tim assured her.

"I'd be very grateful if you could arrange housekeepers. That'll free me up to start making arrangements for my move here," she said.

"Will do. Don't hesitate to call me if you need anything. Do you have children at home?"

"No. My children are grown and gone and I live alone. Correction – I adopted a stray dog two days ago and she and I will be Rosemont's official residents," she added.

If Tim thought it was odd that this accomplished woman was so anxious to abandon a well-ordered life in the social elite, he didn't let on. They parted with his promise to get back to her in the morning with arrangements for the cleaning crew.

Maggie headed back to the Westbury Animal Hospital shortly before five. John Allen led out a buffed-and-fluffed Eve, wearing a proper collar and leash. "Oh, my gosh. I completely forgot about getting them for her. I guess I'm not a very good dog mommy!" she declared ruefully.

"Don't worry about it. Consider them a welcome gift," he said dismissively. "She's in fine shape. She shouldn't have any reactions to her shots. They've got her paperwork and dog food samples at the front desk," he said as Maggie got down on one knee to accept Eve's enthusiastic greeting.

Maggie looked up and flashed a warm smile. "Thank you very much, Dr. Allen."

"Let me know if you need anything or have any questions. You'll be fine. Just stay away from feeding people food," he reminded.

"Will do," she said, smiling back at him over her shoulder as she and Eve headed to the desk.

Dr. John Allen felt an unexpected jolt of happiness as he regarded his new patient and her fascinating owner.

Tim was as good as his word, and at eight o'clock the next morning he called to tell her he would be over in an hour with a cleaning crew to get Rosemont whipped into shape. The crew was composed of four young Amish women. Beautiful girls with clear skin and long hair wound into buns covered with nets.

Evidently they had been working together for some time because they quickly unloaded their supplies and sprang into concerted action without direction from Maggie. Over the next four days, she marveled as Rosemont was transformed from its state of benign neglect to one of gleaming beauty. The lively conversations between these hardworking, cheerful girls brought a sense of vibrancy to the place that had long been missing. She swore she could feel the house smile. Eve, on the other hand, did not like the frequent running of vacuum cleaners and gave the crew a wide berth, preferring to glue herself to Maggie.

Maggie, now totally smitten with her new companion, was anxious to complete the necessary paperwork to secure her adoption. The temperature dropped as the late afternoon faded to dusk and sleet stuck to the ground, making the roads treacherous, as she cautiously entered the parking lot of Forever Friends. I should have turned around and gone back home, she berated herself. I don't know how to drive in this stuff. They wouldn't have given Eve to someone else if I had waited until tomorrow to finalize things. And if I ran into any resistance, that nice Frank Haynes would have smoothed things over for me. Her trusty Uggs provided firm traction across the icy lot. She was standing at a tall counter, filling out forms when a vaguely familiar voice called her name. She turned to see a smiling Frank Haynes coming toward her.

"Mrs. Martin?" he asked as he extended his hand.

"Maggie, please," she replied as she shifted her pen to her left hand and they shook. "I'm getting Eve's adoption finalized. Thank you for smoothing the way for me."

"My pleasure. I heard from Dr. Allen that she checked out just fine. I hope you're enjoying her."

"Absolutely. She's wonderful."

"How are you finding Westbury? Quite a change from southern California, isn't it? Especially on a day like today. Most people want to move *to* California. We don't have many that do it the other way around."

"You're right about the weather, for sure. But don't sell Westbury short. It has a lot of charm. And the people are warm and friendly. Authentic. You've been so nice and helpful to me." Haynes inwardly cursed himself. "And, of course, then there's Rosemont."

"Ah, yes. Rosemont. A big old beauty, to be sure. But sort of an albatross, I would think. What with all of the repair and constant maintenance. Seems like a lot for one woman to take on, if you don't mind me saying."

"Fortunately, I've found a wonderful handyman and we're getting everything in shape. I've only been there a short time, but it's home already. I suspect my moving here will strike people as odd. But it feels right to me."

"Well, time will tell," he said through a tight-lipped smile. "I'll let you get back to your paperwork. We close in ten minutes." And without waiting for further reply, Haynes turned and walked stiffly away.

While Rosemont was being cleaned and polished, Maggie responded to emails from clients, arranged for cable TV and internet service, and added to her lists of things to accomplish both there and in California. Her clients knew she was on vacation this week and she didn't receive many messages from them. She was surprised, however, that she received only a few emails from her "friends" back home. Maggie always suspected that most of them had been centered on Paul, or more specifically on what Paul could do for them. She felt betrayed by the people who turned away from her after the first few weeks of activity following his death. Truth be told, the funeral and reception afterward had been a social occasion and one's place in the local pecking order was determined by how much you did for the family and how close you sat to them at the funeral. Maggie loathed the shallowness of it all. As the week wore on, she realized that it would be far easier to cut ties than she had first thought.

Maggie took photos of each room and made inventories of furniture, rugs, lamps, and accessories. She loved the old-world European style of Rosemont. Generous, comfortable, inviting and livable. She quickly realized than none of her contemporary furnishings in California would be suitable here. And that she was ready for a complete change. It would be much simpler, anyway, to pack up her clothes and her family photos and heirlooms, and leave the rest. A lightness settled on her as she decided to let Mike and Susan take what they wanted and to sell or donate the remainder.

Sam arrived every afternoon by three o'clock and worked his way through leaking plumbing, sagging hinges, and a host of other delayed maintenance items. He always let Maggie know he was there, but he wasn't chatty and worked steadily and methodically through his tasks. Maggie was surprised to see him on Wednesday and assured him it was fine if he quit working early to get ready for the town hall meeting. "I know how important this is to you. Be sure to give that Councilwoman my card. I may be able to refer you to someone who can help."

"I've already passed it on. Tonya said that a forensic accountant is exactly what we need and if we can raise some money to hire one, she'll call you. And to thank you very much."

Maggie's head snapped up. Of course these good people couldn't afford to hire a consultant. She was the person they needed. Here she was, in their midst, about to move into this glorious house she had been lucky enough to inherit. If this wasn't the hand of fate telling her to give back, she didn't know what it was. She checked her watch and decided to finish one more email before she got ready to attend the town hall meeting and do everything in her power to help.

Chapter 4

As she changed clothes for the meeting, Maggie recognized she would be making her Westbury debut and carefully attended to her hair and makeup. She dressed in the black St. John suit she always packed when she needed business attire away from home. Surveying herself in the mirror, she was pleased with the effect. Elegant, classy, and understated. Exactly the tone she wanted to set.

Maggie allowed more than enough time to locate the Library and arrived thirty minutes early. A crowd had already assembled and she got one of the last spots in the parking lot. She wove around clusters of people talking animatedly as she made her way to the entrance. I'm in for quite an interesting evening, Maggie thought. Heads turned in her direction as she passed and a curious buzz followed in her wake.

Maggie caught sight of Sam Torres just as he spotted her. He waved her over to where he and Joan were waiting for the doors to open. They greeted each other warmly. " I can't believe you're here! Are you attending the meeting?" Joan asked.

"Of course I am," Maggie assured her. "This is exactly the kind of thing I investigate in my business. I'm so sorry that I didn't volunteer to help you right away," she apologized. "This is a huge issue. And by the looks of this crowd, it's vitally important to a lot of people. My experience might come in handy here," she offered.

"That's what we were just saying," Joan agreed. "I was hoping you'd help us figure out what's going on."

Their conversation was cut short as the Library's doors swung open and people pushed forward to get out of the frigid evening and find a seat in the overheated main reading room. Maggie trailed closely behind Sam and Joan and they managed to find three seats together in the second row. Chairs were closely spaced and the bulky winter coats that everyone held on their laps added to the cramped feeling. The nape of Maggie's neck was growing damp and she felt a wee bit claustrophobic. She was wishing she hadn't stuck her nose into this whole mess and was home in her pajamas with Eve, when a hush fell on the room and a statuesque dark-haired woman in a tailored navy suit and pearls took the podium. Tonya Holmes had high cheekbones, mahogany skin, and a commanding presence. She waited until the room was absolutely still and all eyes were upon her before she spoke.

"My friends, thank you for coming out on this cold evening. We're a bit crowded in here tonight. That's a good thing. I'm encouraged that so many of you are interested in what's going on. We've got some pretty distressing things to talk about, so make yourselves as comfortable as you can. We've got a water station in the back, so feel free to get up and stretch your legs or get a drink whenever you need to."

She's good, Maggie thought.

Tonya continued in a steady tone, "I promise you that I'll listen to what each of you has to say. And if we run out of time tonight, we'll hold another town hall meeting. Everyone will be heard. And no matter what we uncover in our investigation, we'll get through this together in a way that best serves all of us. Westbury has a long, proud heritage of selfless community action and we're going to continue that tradition. I grew up here; fourth generation. I've known all of the powers to be all of my life. *And I am not scared of any of them.* I'm staying right here until the job is done," she declared forcefully.

At this, the crowd began to clap, at first tentatively in that space that was usually so quiet, then growing in enthusiasm. The energy in the room was palpable.

"Now," Tonya said, "As you know, I have been calling for an independent audit of Westbury's books. At first, I simply thought this was a good practice. I never dreamed that something could be wrong. But the more I requested and pushed for one, the more the Mayor and the other Council Members balked and stalled and misdirected the conversation."

"I grew up the oldest child in a large family," she continued. "I've heard plenty of wild excuses and tall tales in my time. My mother always knew when one of us was lying, and I guess I've inherited her nose for nonsense." At this, a chuckle rippled through the crowd. "I felt like I was back in my mother's kitchen with my brothers when these guys were making excuses to avoid an audit," she said. "So I got my back up and decided that I was going to find out about the town's finances one way or the other. And at last week's Town Council meeting I finally got my chance. Mayor Wheeler left the bank statement out on the Council table in plain sight when we went to recess." Tonya paused for dramatic effect. "So I spent my recess pouring through it. Long story short, the general account is about half of what was reported in the treasurer's report and the pension fund was short by almost forty percent," she announced, as a gasp escaped from the crowd.

Side conversations started up all over the room. Tonya raised her hands and gestured for quiet. "At this point, I don't have a good picture of where the money has gone. I confronted the Mayor and Council when we resumed after recess. They scolded me for looking at 'confidential Town information', as they called it, telling me that I didn't understand what I was looking at. 'Well, enlighten me,' I said. Instead, they quickly adjourned the meeting. I've been calling the Mayor and each of my fellow Council Members ever since and no one has been available to take my call. And they're not coming to their offices, either."

"They've all gone to ground," she continued. "And you hunters in the crowd know what that means. We have to drive them out of their hidey-holes. And this is where I desperately need your help. Each and every one of you."

"First, I need everyone in this room to contact the Mayor and their Council Member, demanding an immediate audit of the Town's financials. You can do this by phone, fax, letter or email. I want them inundated with demands. They need to know that they cannot escape this issue. I've put a list of the contact information you'll need on handouts for you to pick up on the way out."

"Second, we need to be able to quickly communicate with each other. I want to know what response you're getting from them. I'd like to be the gathering point for information. The handout has all of my contact numbers. I'm going to send out email updates. If you'd like to receive them, put your email address on the sheet that's being circulated."

"Lastly, I need a small committee of volunteers to analyze the information that we receive and formulate a strategy to deal with whatever we uncover. That should be the Town Council's job, but I don't think we can rely on them. Former prosecutor Alex Scanlon has agreed to help us. I'd also like to have a CPA, a business owner, and one representative from the teacher's union and one from the Town workers' union. So if you're interested in serving, or know someone who would be good, please see me after," she stated.

"I know that this is all very upsetting, but as I said in the beginning, none of us are going anywhere so we better figure this out and fix it together. Your coming here tonight has been very encouraging to me," she said with a catch in her voice. "I love Westbury and am so proud to be on the Town Council. I look forward to continuing to serve you," she concluded.

The crowd began to clap. Sam was the first person on his feet and the rest of the room followed suit with a rousing ovation. Tonya flushed and discretely dabbed at the corner of her eye with a tissue. She certainly has guts to stand up to the old boy network, Maggie thought with admiration.

When the applause died down and the crowd began to disburse, Maggie made her way to the podium. She introduced herself and told Tonya that she had just relocated to Westbury, was a forensic accountant and would serve on the committee.

Tonya looked visibly relieved. "This is great news. Sam gave me your card. I was hoping we could get you to help. Since you're just moving here, I didn't think there was any way that you'd have the time or the interest. I don't know what to say. I'm very grateful."

Maggie dismissed her thanks with an embarrassed wave and told her that she would be in California the next week, but would make herself available for conference calls with the committee and would be available via email. Around the clock, if that was what the situation required. "Don't worry, we'll figure this out," she assured Tonya as she stepped aside to make way for the crowd gathering around the Councilwoman.

"Why, hello, Dr. Allen," Tonya greeted John warmly as he approached. "I thought I saw you in the crowd. Thank you for making the time to come," she said.

"Wouldn't have missed it," he assured her. "If you don't have another business owner in mind for your committee, I'd be happy to help you. This issue affects all of us in many ways."

"Terrific. I now have three members of my committee. Have you met Maggie Martin?" Tonya asked. "She's new in Town and is a forensic accountant," she said as she turned to Maggie.

Maggie and John smiled at each other and John said that they had just met, that Maggie's dog was one of his patients. Tonya regarded them thoughtfully. "Great. We're off to a good start." At this point, Sam leaned in and offered to be the Town worker's union representative. He pointed to Maggie and said, "Didn't I tell you? She's going to help us, isn't she? She's exactly what we need."

"Absolutely," Tonya replied. "For a newcomer, you sure know a lot of people," Tonya observed. She turned to address a question from a young woman who had been patiently waiting her turn, as Maggie, Sam and John drifted over to the door where Joan was waiting.

"I'm returning to California on Sunday to make arrangements for my move here," Maggie told them. "I don't plan to be gone too long. I'm hoping to be back in a week. I'm used to working remotely, so I can do my part," she assured them.

John looked at her quizzically. He didn't say anything but was thinking what a dynamo she must be if she could pack up her life and move across the country in one week's time, all the while maintaining her business and helping on this committee. "Why don't we get together as a group once before you leave," he suggested. "Meet at Pete's, my treat," he offered. "I'll get with Tonya and set something up."

With this decided, they headed out into the night. Freezing rain made the parking lot treacherous, especially in the dress heels that Maggie wore. She slipped and caught herself on the side mirror of a parked car. John took her elbow and, ignoring her embarrassed protests, steered her steadily to her car.

"Thank you so much," she blushed. "I guess I need to watch the weather before I pick out my shoes."

"You don't get freezing rain in southern California too often, do you? You'll get used to it. How's Eve doing?" he asked. "No reaction to the shots?"

"None," Maggie replied. "She doesn't much like vacuum cleaners, but other than that, she's very happy. I was going to call your office to board her with you while I'm in California."

"We'll take good care of her while you're gone. No worries," he said.

Maggie heaved a sigh of relief. "I'll feel better about leaving her with you. I'll call in the morning," she said as she got into her car. She watched him walk away as she pulled out of the lot.

Chapter 5

Frank Haynes was sitting at his desk early the next morning, studying the spreadsheet detailing the terms of his restaurant leases. He was pleased with what he saw; he had really been able to put it to those greedy-bastard landlords in this recession. He relaxed into his large leather chair as he swiveled to answer the phone.

"Frank, is that you?" the man asked in a throaty whisper.

Haynes' congenial mood evaporated. "What?"

"I went to that meeting at the Library last night, like you said. That Holmes bitch knows the accounts are short. She's stirring up people to hound the Council for an audit. She's formed a committee to look into stuff."

"Shit. We knew this could happen. We've got contingency plans in place. And a bunch of local yokels aren't going to be able to figure this out," Haynes replied.

"They're not all local yokels, Frank. They've got Scanlon on the committee. He may be a fag, but he was one tough mother when he was a prosecutor. And you can't shake off that Holmes broad."

"Who else do they have?"

"Not sure if this is everybody, but it looks like an old broad teacher, that school janitor guy Torres who does handyman work, the vet – he's smart – and some new broad. I think she must be the CPA they said they wanted."

Haynes cocked one eyebrow. Was Maggie Martin sticking her nose in this? What a pain in the ass she was turning out to be.

"Frank? That's all I found out. Expect to get calls from your constituents today."

"You did good. Thank you."

"Anything else you want me to do?"

"No – not yet," and Haynes slowly replaced the receiver.

Getting Mrs. Martin out of Rosemont and headed back to California was looking more attractive all the time. What was it they said about keeping friends close and enemies closer? He'd have to keep an eye on her.

Chapter 6

Maggie rose early on Saturday and dropped Eve off at the Westbury Animal Hospital. It was hard to say which one was more anxious and miserable about being apart. Maggie was grateful that she had the committee meeting at Pete's to take her mind off of their parting.

She walked through the door of Pete's Bistro at ten minutes before eight. The place was getting busy with people running weekend errands, joggers, and dog walkers taking a break. She introduced herself to the man behind the counter. Pete Fitzpatrick greeted her warmly and said he had heard a lot about her from his wife and from Dr. Allen. "Your meeting is in the room on the right at the top of the stairs," he told her. "You're the first to arrive. We've got a full breakfast for you up there," he added.

Maggie skirted a young couple soothing a fussy baby and made her way up the stairs. The heady aroma of coffee and bacon lead her to the small, utilitarian meeting room. She was pouring herself a cup when Tonya burst into the room juggling an unruly stack of papers and a briefcase. Maggie quickly set her cup down and rushed over to grab them before they escaped from Tonya's arms.

"I just picked up copies of bank statements for the last two years," Tonya declared triumphantly. "The Town Clerk evidently doesn't look kindly on the fact that her pension might be in jeopardy. I haven't had a chance to go through them yet. I made an extra copy and was hoping you might review them when you get back," she continued.

"I'll do better than that," Maggie replied. "I'm itching to see what's going on. I'll have six hours on the plane to read them tomorrow. I won't be able to put together a comprehensive report in that time, but I'll have some preliminary conclusions. I'll call you when I land, if you like," she offered.

"Perfect," Tonya replied. "The sooner the better."

Both women turned at the sound of approaching footsteps. John and Sam came through the door together, followed by a neat man in his early thirties with a trim build and precise haircut. He said hello to Tonya and introduced himself to Maggie as Alex Scanlon.

"He's the attorney on our committee," Tonya said. "We've got the smartest, hardest-working one in the state on our side," she added. Alex shrugged off the compliment, but Maggie could see he was pleased. "And here comes Beth," she continued as a stout, grey-haired woman in sensible shoes entered the room. "Everyone, this is Beth O'Malley. She teaches economics and civics at the high school and is our representative from the teacher's union. Why don't you get your breakfast, courtesy of John, and let's get started."

As they filled their plates and crowded around the small table, Tonya reported that the switchboard at Town Hall was swamped on Thursday and Friday with citizens calling the Mayor or their Council Member to request an audit. "I think all of this attention has those boys spooked," she said. "The mood is somber. No more of their self-satisfied swagger."

She added that she had a source within Town Hall, an employee sympathetic to their cause. The Mayor must not find out that this person was feeding them information or they could lose their job. "Our source gave us bank statements. Maggie has agreed to take a first pass through them on her flight back to California tomorrow. She's going to call me tomorrow night with her preliminary conclusions. I'll be in touch with all of you Monday and we'll decide what our next steps should be."

"What else can we do right now?" Beth asked. "I'm feeling fairly useless."

Alex stated that there wasn't much to do at the moment. "We need to be very cautious and make sure that we have all of the facts before we take action. I think the calls to the Mayor and Council are an excellent start. They won't be able to orchestrate a cover up now. Maggie's got all of the work at the moment," he said.

"I understand how important this issue is and my assistance to this committee is my top priority. You don't know me yet, but you can count on me. I'll be gone for a week or ten days, at the most. And I'll have my cell phone on me at all times, so you can always reach me."

With that, the meeting adjourned. John grabbed the stack of copies off of the table and, despite Maggie's protest that she didn't need any help, carried them to her car. "We all appreciate your jumping into this mess," he said.

"This is what I do for a living and, frankly, I'm good at it. You need my expertise. And I want to make Westbury my home; I want to feel connected, to be useful. I'm sorry for the circumstances, but I'm grateful to have a project that will allow me to make my mark."

"You'll also be making some enemies – powerful enemies – you realize that, don't you?" he cautioned.

Maggie truthfully hadn't thought about that but assured him that she wasn't concerned. "I'm off," she said, as she climbed into her car. "See you soon. Take good care of Eve. I miss her already."

Chapter 7

By the time Maggie landed at LAX early the next afternoon, she had reached solid conclusions and was anxious to relay them to Tonya.

Maggie called Susan and Mike from her car to let them know she was safely home and invited them to dinner the next night. She needed to tell them about her move and get them thinking about what they wanted from the house. They both acquiesced after she insisted that it couldn't wait until the weekend. Maggie made a quick stop at the grocery and pulled into the familiar driveway shortly after three o'clock.

The house seemed cold and almost accusatory when she stepped through the side door with her purchases. It knew, she thought. She was surprised that she wasn't glad to be there. She wandered from room to room, looking at the familiar furnishings, trying to feel something; anything. The sleek leather sofa that had been so inviting no longer beckoned. The slate floors and chic grey walls seemed sterile; the glass tabletops antiseptic. It was no longer home. Any doubts about her move to Rosemont evaporated.

Maggie spent the next hour going through the house, making lists of things to pack. She would get boxes and bubble wrap the next morning.

Promptly at five o'clock, Maggie spread the bank statements out on her dining room table and dialed Tonya. She answered on the second ring. "Well?" she asked, skipping any polite small talk.

Maggie launched into her conclusions. "The Town's revenue has declined over the past two years and appears to have stabilized, with an increasing trend for the last six months. That's the good news," she said. "The main operating account appears to pay legitimate expenses, with the exception of monthly transfers in large amounts – between ten and one hundred thousand dollars each – to offshore accounts."

"First I've heard of that," Tonya huffed. "There can't be any legitimate reason for that."

"I agree. We need to find out about those accounts – their ownership – and where the money goes from there. We'll need Alex's help with that. At least we have the account numbers and depository institutions. We're at a standstill until we get more information. But I believe this confirms our suspicions that someone is embezzling," she concluded.

"I can guess who," Tonya insisted. "Wheeler and Delgado, for sure. The Council is probably all dirty. Except maybe Frank Haynes. He's an odd duck, to be sure. I don't know if he's in on it or not. He's been on the Council for at least a decade, but he keeps to himself. Just sits on the Council, runs his fast-food franchises, and supports the no-kill animal shelter. Anyone who loves animals that much can't be all bad. Anyway, I'm half tempted to confront them all right now," she spat.

"No," Maggie cautioned. "That would be very foolish. We need more information. And this is definitely big-time criminal activity. Could they be mob connected?" she asked.

"There have been rumors of that for years," Tonya said. "You're right. I need to keep a cool head for now and sit on this while we keep digging," she agreed. "What did you see with respect to the pension account?"

"The deposits to that account have decreased as the Town's revenue has decreased, but the contributions have remained at the same percentage of revenue. So I don't think that the funding of the account is a problem," she stated. "The Treasurer's report states that the value of the assets in the account is way down. Most investments have been hurt by the recession, so it's hard to tell whether the decline is due to ordinary market risk or whether the investments made by the pension fund were poor or inappropriate," she concluded. "And since we don't know what the pension fund is invested in, we can't assess whether those investments are likely to recover as the economy improves. Do you have an outside investment advisor for the pension fund, and is the fund audited?" she asked.

"I wish," Tonya said angrily. "The investment manager is Wheeler's brother-in-law, Ron Delgado. I'll bet that the pension fund is 'invested' in the business interests of Wheeler, Delgado, the Council and their cronies. This whole thing makes me furious. The Town employees get an annual report about the pension fund," she stated. "I'll get copies to you and Alex."

"Be very discrete," Maggie warned. "We're starting to pull on a thread and we don't know what it will unravel. Someone's been embezzling for years and won't look kindly on this investigation. One more thing may work in our favor. If they've been doing this for years, they've probably gotten sloppy in covering their tracks. Someone may have slipped up somewhere, and that will help us find out what's been going on," she concluded.

"From your lips to God's ears," Tonya said. "And you're right. I'll be careful."

"I'll drop what I'm doing here to review anything you can get hold of," she promised. "This is going to take time to straighten out. Don't do anything rash," she repeated.

Maggie slept uneasily. She woke frequently, worried about the corruption in Westbury. And she missed the sweet comfort of Eve's presence at her feet.

Despite her restless night, Maggie woke early, full of energy. By noon she had decided what to take to Rosemont and had made arrangements for movers to come on Wednesday. She signed listing papers on her house that afternoon, with the sign to go in the yard by the end of the week. Fortunately, the house and yard were in good shape and the minor repairs and touch-ups would be handled by her realtor after she returned to Westbury.

Maggie decided it was time to set the stage for the nice dinner she had planned for Mike and Susan. This would be her last party in this house, she realized wistfully. She reflected back on all of the entertaining she had done, most of it supporting Paul's career. Intimate dinners with colleagues, receptions for alumni donors, brunches for academics. They hosted something at least once a

56

week. She prided herself on her ability to conjure up a meal for fifty on a moment's notice. Maggie had a short list of specialty shops that could be counted on to supply breads, desserts, and appetizers. They didn't have the budget for a caterer, so Maggie did all of the planning and most of the cooking herself. She loved throwing a party and knew she had a well-deserved reputation for hospitality. It was disorienting when all of that activity came to a screeching halt after Paul's death. She remembered the fabulous kitchen at Rosemont and promised herself that she would form a new circle of friends, this time centered on her interests, and reestablish herself in Westbury.

Maggie placed a rib roast in the oven and set about making an apple pie. She peeled potatoes and put them on the stove to boil. This situation required comfort food, to be sure. The soothing aroma of a home-cooked meal bolstered her. Although she hated to admit it, she was apprehensive about telling her children that she was selling the house and moving to Westbury. Whose life was it, anyway? As she worked, she rehearsed what she wanted to say to them.

Mike barged into the kitchen promptly at six o'clock, declaring, "Something smells good!" He swept his mother into a hug that lifted her off her feet. She choked back tears as she placed a kiss on each cheek. "You ok, mom?" he asked as held her at arms' length. She nodded and motioned for him to open the wine he had brought and pour them both a glass. They were catching up on the news of the twins when Susan blew through the door in her typical rush of apologies for being late, lamenting how busy she was at work. Mike rolled his eyes and handed her a glass of wine.

"So, mom, tell us all about Rosemont," Susan commanded.

"It's a mini Downton Abbey. Photos don't do it justice, but they'll have to suffice," Maggie said and lead them through the snapshots she had loaded onto her laptop. They were suitably stunned and impressed.

"This is absolutely magnificent," Susan gasped. "Why do you think dad never mentioned his family in Westbury? And why did he never tell us he inherited Rosemont?" she asked. "It must be worth a tidy sum."

"Knowing dad, he probably wanted to take us all there as a surprise. But he never got the chance," Mike observed sadly.

Maggie had repeatedly asked herself these same questions, but she suspected his reasons for keeping Rosemont and the small fortune associated with it a secret were not so honorable. She buried these thoughts and continued, "The people in Westbury are warm and friendly and genuine. When I was there I felt a peacefulness and purposefulness that I haven't felt in months," she stated. She quickly continued, before she lost her nerve, "I think Westbury is the perfect place for the fresh start I've been craving."

At this statement, both children looked at Maggie intently. She held her breath and looked calmly back at them.

"What do you mean, mom? Fresh start? I don't get it," Susan finally replied.

"You know how awkward things have been for me with the College crowd. The new President and his wife are headed in a different direction and don't want me hanging around. I don't feel like I fit anywhere anymore. Helen is the only friend that I continue to see," she said. Maggie raised her hand to hush their objections. "You both have your own lives. I need to have mine. I can run my business from anywhere with a phone and a computer."

"So you're thinking of moving there?" Susan choked.

"That's exactly what I've decided to do," Maggie replied with her best attempt at a firm, confident voice.

"But you don't know anyone there," Susan protested.

"Won't you rattle around in that huge house all alone? Won't that make you feel more alone?" Mike interjected for the first time.

"You know, that's the part I'm most sure of. That I won't be lonely in that house. When the front door closed behind me that first night, I knew I was home. I never told you, but I checked out of the hotel and moved into Rosemont the night I arrived," Maggie said. Mike and Susan exchanged a skeptical glance. "And you know, the most extraordinary thing happened the next morning. I adopted a lost dog. Or more accurately, she adopted me," Maggie said, and told them about Eve. "So you see, I won't be alone there," Maggie finished.

Both children remained silent. Astonished, Maggie thought with a measure of satisfaction.

"I didn't even know you liked dogs," Susan muttered.

"Your dad was such a dominant character," Maggie stated. "There are a lot of things that I gave up rather than argue with him about," she said. "Pets were one of those things."

"What about the twins," Mike asked. "You adore each other. They'll be devastated. I can't believe that you would move so far away from them."

"I've thought a lot about that," Maggie said. "I travel on business all the time. I'll be out here at least one week a month. I'll probably see them as much as I do now. And they can come spend summer vacations with me and we'll have a lot of old-fashioned fun that they don't have now," she added. "Being exposed to a different part of the country will be good for them. For both of you, too"

"So when do you plan to do all of this? Just up and leave us?" Susan pouted.

"Maybe you should try it out for a few months to see if you like it." Mike suggested reasonably.

"I've volunteered to assist the Town Council with an accounting matter," Maggie stated, glossing over the severity of the matter. "I'll need to get back to Westbury as soon as possible. I've had Rosemont cleaned and hooked up to cable and internet, so it's ready to go. This house is too much of a handful to hang onto as a second home. It's also too full of memories of your dad. You know that I've been toying with the idea of selling it and have decided to do that. I've listed it for sale and am having movers pack up what I want to take to Rosemont," she said. "I'll rent a place closer to the two of you," she continued quickly. "And maybe you can keep your eyes peeled for a nice townhouse that I can purchase to be my home out here," she concluded.

"I'm just shocked," Susan sniffed. The tears she had been holding back broke free. "I think this is impetuous and stupid. We need you here. If you want to give this hair-brained idea a try, do it; but don't sell this house yet."

Mike nodded in agreement. "No need to rush into this. Just hang onto your house for now. You can buy something else later."

"I considered that," Maggie said. "I've thought about this long and hard. I've always supported the two of you in your decisions, haven't I?" She looked pointedly at both of her children and could see that she had hit her mark. " I've decided to sell this house now. I need a clean slate."

Susan turned away but Mike nodded and took Maggie's hand. Encouraged, she continued, "I don't want any of this furniture. I want the two of you to take anything and everything you'd like to have. The more the better. Anything that you don't want, I'll sell or donate," she said. "There's no real rush. My stuff will be out of here on Wednesday. The realtor will have someone stage the house on Friday. You can come by any time to select what you want. I only ask that you be fair to each other and don't make a mess for the realtor."

"Well, duh, mom," Susan said with an impatient shake of her head.

"We just want you to be happy," Mike sighed. "If this is what you want, we'll do whatever we can to help you. You can always come back if it doesn't work out. Nothing's permanent."

"And thank you for letting us take things from the house," Susan snuffled. "I love some of this stuff."

Maggie smiled at the two faces she cherished most in the world. They were wonderful children and things were going to work out just fine.

Chapter 8

The remainder of the week flew by for Maggie. Wednesday was chaotic with movers packing and loading all day. She decided to ship her car to Westbury and keep Paul's car to use in California. The twins had an early release day from school on Thursday and Mike brought them over to Maggie's so she could spend the afternoon with them. The day was clear and mild, so Maggie took Sarah and Sophie to the park near her house.

She planted herself on a bench and turned her face to the sun. The happy shouts of her beloved granddaughters and the occasional "Gramma, watch this!" filled the space. How dreadfully she would miss this; maybe her kids were right. Maybe this move was ill-conceived. Maggie abruptly stood up and strode onto the playground.

"It's not time to go, is it?" Sophie asked, surprised that her grandmother was coming toward them.

"No. Not even close. I just need a hug," Maggie said as she scooped her into an embrace and Sophie nestled close.

"Gramma, push me!" Sarah called.

"Come on, Sophie. I can push both of you."

They set off for home, hand-in-hand, when the sun slanted low through the trees. Over the girls' favorite dinner of mac and cheese and hot dogs, Maggie asked if their dad told them she was moving to a great big house in Westbury. They nodded sullenly. "Don't be sad," Maggie said with a brightness she didn't feel. "I'll come here all the time for business and we'll see each other as much as ever," she assured them. "My new house is so big and grand it even has a name. Rosemont. Everyone in town knows the house by its name," she informed them.

"Like a castle?" Sophie asked. "Does it have a drawbridge and moat and stuff?" Sarah chimed in.

Maggie smiled. "Not quite like a castle. It's not that old. No moat or drawbridge, but lots of nooks and crannies." They were quiet as they considered this. "Would you like to come visit me there this summer? You could help me explore the house and the big yard around it," she added.

This definitely hit a respondent cord. "Oh, could we?" Sarah breathed. "That would be fun," Sophie agreed.

"Absolutely," Maggie said. "There are five extra bedrooms – you can take your pick and you can share one or each have your own room. And you can meet my new dog, Eve," she added.

"You have a dog?" both girls cried at once. "Daddy didn't tell us," they said rather indignantly.

"Yes. You'll love her. She's a doll. You can take her on walks and play with her. She'll adore you," Maggie promised. "Let me show you photos," she said as she opened her laptop and brought up pictures of Rosemont and Eve. They were full of questions about both, but Eve was definitely the bigger attraction. "The one thing Rosemont doesn't have is toys," Maggie continued. "So when you come, we'll have to go out and buy new ones to keep at my house." And with this happy prospect before them, Maggie sealed the deal. They would most definitely visit this summer.

Maggie finished the week with an impromptu going-away party thrown for her on Sunday afternoon by Helen Farley, the one friend she would sorely miss. Helen and Maggie ran in the same circles and had many common acquaintances. The turn out was good and Maggie was satisfied that she got to say goodbye. She could sense the unspoken astonishment at her decision to pull up stakes. She didn't supply any details about her new home and skillfully sidestepped the occasional intrusive question. The exception to this was Helen; she gave Helen the whole story, including her intention to return frequently on business and rent or buy a place in the area. "Okay," Helen said. "I'm not going to pretend to understand all this, but I've known you long enough to know when you've made up your mind. I'll miss you terribly. You better keep your promise to stay in touch," she added tearfully. Maggie hugged Helen long and hard and promised that she would hardly notice that Maggie had moved.

Susan picked Maggie up the next morning to take her to the airport. She was sullen and uninterested in small talk. When they parked at the terminal, Maggie turned to Susan. "I know this is sudden and difficult. It is for me, too. I know you and your brother will be fine with me a bit further away. I wouldn't be doing this otherwise. I could never start over again and form a new life for myself if I stayed here. I've always supported you in your dreams," she said, turning to look directly at Susan. "I now expect you to support me in mine."

Susan sighed heavily. "You're right, mom. I know you are. And you know that I love you and want you to be happy. I guess it's just a little scary for me to be so far away from you," she said with an embarrassed laugh. "I may be a high-powered litigator, but I guess part of me still wants my mom around." Susan smiled at Maggie. It was Maggie's turn to swallow her tears. "Let's get your suitcase out of the trunk before we both start blubbering," Susan said.

They walked to the security checkpoint going over the details that would fill the next week for each of them. "I'll be back before you know it," Maggie assured her. They held their hug a bit longer than usual. Maggie picked up her carryon, and turned toward her future.

Chapter 9

Maggie's flight arrived late and she hurried to the rental car company. She was relieved that there was no line and she was able to walk right up to the counter. Her hopes of getting on her way quickly, however, were dashed by an agent in a talkative mood. He didn't take the hint from Maggie's clipped answers that she was in a hurry. She did her best to act with patience she didn't feel, and snatched the keys from his hands when he finally held them out to her. She firmly declined his offer to review the features of the car and headed to the lot at a trot.

If she made really good time, she would get to the Westbury Animal Hospital in time to pick up Eve. Maggie was anxious to see her new companion and was equally as anxious to avoid a night at Rosemont alone. She called the Hospital from the car and said she was on her way but might be a few minutes late. The young man told her that he had to leave on time that night but that Dr. Allen was usually there for a while after closing and would probably let her pick up her pet. He promised to let Dr. Allen know she was on her way.

Maggie concentrated on the drive. This was no time to miss her exit. She arrived in the parking lot at twenty minutes after six. The lot was empty and her heart sank. She stumbled as she hurried to the door and it was flung open, and an ecstatic Eve bounded out to greet her.

Maggie dropped to her knees and threw her arms around the squirming dog. "You don't know how much I appreciate being able to have Eve with me tonight," she beamed up at John. "My flight was delayed and I had a Chatty-Cathy car rental agent. I drove like a maniac to get here. I'm really very grateful you waited. The lot was empty and I thought that I was too late."

"It was no trouble. I was catching up on paperwork," John assured her. "I live on the other side of the Square and walk to work, weather permitting. I usually stop at one of the restaurants on the way home for dinner."

"Are you done? Would you like a lift home?"

John knew an opportunity when he saw one. "I just need to lock up," he said. "Are you hungry? Or are you full of delicious airline food," he mocked. When she shook her head and indicated that she was, indeed, starved, he proposed that the three of them walk over to Pete's for dinner. They could leave her car at the Hospital and she could drop him off at his house after dinner.

Pete tucked the three of them into a cozy table by the window. Only a handful of the other tables were occupied, but Pete was doing a robust weeknight takeout business. The special was old-fashioned baked ziti with homemade bread and a salad. A sign announced that customers could add Laura's pie of the day – which today was blueberry – for five dollars more. "I wish I could have fed my family at Pete's when my kids were little," Maggie idly mused.

John helped Maggie out of her coat and she relaxed back into her chair. Eve curled up at their feet. She ordered rainbow trout and a house salad. John opted for salmon on a cedar plank and a cup of homemade vegetable soup. While they waited for their food, Maggie filled John in on her preliminary conclusions from her review of the bank statements.

John whistled softly. "We've got trouble in River City, that's for sure," he said. "I know a pretty fair percentage of the people in this Town," he continued. "Hard-working, decent people who take care of their families, their homes and their neighbors. Give-you-the-shirt-off-of-their backs kind of folks. We can't let a few crooks ruin what so many have worked so hard for. I won't stand by and let that happen."

"I'm looking forward to getting together with the committee again. I'm sorry that the subject is so dire, but it's helping me meet people and makes me feel useful," she added. John considered this silently.

"I was always so busy helping Paul with the social obligations of his job," Maggie resumed. "We had something on the calendar almost every night of the week. Paul used to say that if they gave awards for best supporting actress in real life, I would win hands down." As she said this, Maggie realized that Paul hadn't said that for many years. And she wasn't so sure that being the best supporting actress in someone else's life was such a compliment, anyway. Maybe she was just a really good doormat. She shifted uncomfortably and continued, "After Paul's death, all that stopped. The college got a new President and he and his wife took over. I've been feeling adrift. I have a lot of energy and have time on my hands. Tonya Holmes really impressed me. I'm looking forward to helping her."

John smiled. "So tell me more about this mysterious Maggie Martin that's just blown into town."

"Believe me – I am not the least bit mysterious," she replied with a laugh. She told him about her education, her consulting business, her kids, and her childhood. He kept her talking through the main course and into the piece of blueberry pie they agreed to split. His question about what she liked to do for fun caused her to pause. "You know, I'm not sure." She smiled ruefully. "Most of our free time was focused on activities connected with the college. I'm not really sure that I enjoyed a whole lot of it. I was too involved in the doing of it all," she admitted.

John looked into her eyes and waited patiently for her to continue. "To be honest, I'm glad to be making a fresh start in Westbury," she said. "I didn't feel at home last week in California. My only second thoughts are about leaving my granddaughters. But I'll be back on business regularly and will see them almost as much as I ever did. I guess that should tell me something. Shouldn't it be hard to turn your back on a life you've spent more than twenty years living?" she asked with a shrug.

"I've monopolized the whole conversation," she continued apologetically. "I've been around self-absorbed people my whole life, who do just that. I positively hate it. And now I've done it! I'd like to know more about you, John," she said. "Were you born and raised here?"

John looked at his watch as he snatched the check from Pete. "I'd be happy to tell you about myself, but it's getting late. I think

66

that discussion will have to wait. How about we do something Saturday night?" he asked. "Maybe it's time you found out what you like to do for fun? Is there anything that comes to mind, or do you want me to surprise you?" he asked.

Incredibly, she heard herself accepting in a voice that sounded absolutely giddy. "Surprise me," she added, to her further astonishment. Maggie barely paid attention to their conversation as they strolled through the cold night to collect her car. Her mind was racing as she realized that she had just accepted her first date in more than twenty years.

Chapter 10

Maggie slept long and hard, and the sun was pouring in through the cracks in the shutters, when she reluctantly pushed herself up and out of bed the next morning. She fed Eve and took her coffee into the library to set priorities on her "to do" list; find a good dry cleaner; find a gym; find a new nail tech. The list was long. She needed to prepare a report for a client. And she wanted to check with her realtor to see if her California house had any showings over the weekend.

Maggie was hunting for the realtor's card when she heard a car on the drive. She looked out the library window to see Sam pulling up to her mailbox and stuffing a large envelop into it. She rapped on the window and motioned to the door. He removed his parcel from the mailbox and met her at the door.

"Good morning," he said cheerfully. "Tonya told me you'd be back and asked me to bring you these reports on the pension plan for the last seven years. That's all we've kept," he added apologetically.

"That's wonderful, Sam," Maggie assured him. "Most people don't keep any of this. I've got a ton of client work today, but I'll crack them open tonight. I was going to call you," she added. "I'd like to tackle the kitchen first. It needs new appliances and a coat of paint, but the cabinets and countertops are fine, don't you think?" Sam agreed and Maggie continued. "Where would you suggest I go to buy them, and can you install them if I have them delivered?"

"Mayfair Appliance on Sycamore has all the high-end stuff you'll want," Sam replied. "Why don't you pick them out and let me buy them with my contractor's discount. I can install everything. I don't have any extra work scheduled right now, so I can start painting as soon as you decide on the color. Go down to Westbury Hardware – they're two blocks south of the Library – and select your color. I'll pick it up after school and get started. Or whenever you have time," he added hastily.

"Perfect. I'm anxious to get going on this. Pencil me in for every afternoon until we get Rosemont up to snuff. If you get called out on an emergency for another client, I'll understand. Everything I want to have done can be put off, if necessary."

Sam was delighted at the prospect of a steady stream of work. And Maggie was glad that she could help supply some of his much-needed supplemental income.

With the happy prospect of shopping for home improvements on her agenda, Maggie dove into the report she promised her client and pushed the send button on her email just before noon. Anxious to begin putting her own stamp on Rosemont, she headed out to Westbury Hardware.

As she considered colors and selected paint chips to take home, her mind kept returning to her upcoming dinner with John. He was certainly an interesting man. She found herself listing his attributes as if he were a sales prospect: calm, an animal lover (obviously), smart (well, he was a doctor, after all), articulate, concerned about others, probably financially well off, fun, easy to talk to, comfortable to be with, and darned good looking. And interested in her. Or was he? She thought so, but maybe she had been out of circulation so long that she couldn't really tell anymore. Maybe she was just kidding herself? And was she ready to date again? Did she ever want to date again? She had been telling herself that she would never get involved with another man after finding out that she barely knew Paul after all those years of marriage. And yet here she was, daydreaming about a man she barely knew like she was in high school. She forced her attention back to the stack of paint chips she was holding with the thought that maybe John wouldn't follow up about this weekend. Maybe she didn't have anything to worry about after all.

She returned home and after careful consideration of her options, left a message for Sam that she wanted her kitchen to be painted a warm beige called "Toasted Coconut" and had selected a soft yellow with the happy name "Yellow Ducky" for her bedroom. Sam arrived shortly before five with the paint in hand and began to prep the kitchen while Maggie retreated to the library to work.

Chapter 11

A lex Scanlon planned to spend his day preparing a motion for summary judgment. He had no client appointments scheduled and was looking forward to a day of research and writing. He was good at both and enjoyed them.

He opened the large envelope that had been shoved through the mail slot of his office. As Tonya promised, it contained copies of the pension plan annual reports. He put them on the corner of his desk and took one of them into the break room to thumb through while the coffee brewed. By the time he filled his cup and returned to his desk, he was hooked. He spent the rest of the day pouring through the papers, compiling notes and making lists of items to follow up on. His assistant said goodnight hours ago. He took off his glasses, rubbed his tired eyes and placed a call to Maggie.

"Maggie? This is Alex Scanlon. Tonya said you'd be back in town. I've spent the day looking at the pension fund reports. Have you had a chance to review them yet?"

Maggie replied that she had just started and asked him if he had come to any conclusions. Alex let out a heavy sigh and spent the next thirty minutes going over his notes. Maggie listened attentively and interrupted him only occasionally for clarification. "I don't want to sway your analysis," he said. "But I don't think the information can be interpreted any other way."

"I don't think so either," Maggie agreed. "I'll get through this material tonight and I'll call you in the morning if I disagree with you or have anything to add. Assuming I corroborate your conclusions, we need to bring this information to the committee as soon as possible."

"If I haven't heard from you by ten tomorrow morning, I'll call Tonya," Alex said.

"You sound exhausted," Maggie observed. "There's nothing more to do tonight. Go home, try to relax and get a good night's sleep," Maggie added in a motherly tone as they hung up.

Tonya Holmes arrived at Scanlon & Ryan shortly before five on Wednesday. She wanted to copy an agenda and set out materials before the committee arrived at five-thirty. The call from Alex the morning before had confirmed their worst fears. She wondered if this small group could tackle what appeared to be ingrained and pervasive corruption in the Town's government.

Beth was the next to arrive, toting homemade hummus and crudités for the group to snack on. She set her refreshments in the center of the conference table and went in search of the coffee maker to brew a fresh pot.

Sam and Maggie pulled in right after each other at five-thirty. Alex's assistant told them that he was wrapping up a call and would be right in. Maggie doodled on her agenda and kept an anxious eye on the door, watching for John. He had not arrived by the time Alex joined them at five forty-five.

Tonya thanked them all for coming and invited Maggie to recap her conclusions from her review of the bank statements. Everyone listened attentively. The mood in the room was somber. Tonya then turned the floor over to Alex to report on the pension fund.

"Maggie and I both reviewed the paperwork. We've reached the same conclusion. The fund currently manages slightly in excess of forty million dollars in assets. As you know, Ron Delgado is the investment advisor. The pension fund has never had an independent audit. Delgado ran the pension fund like his own piggy bank," Alex stated.

"He invested the pension fund heavily in commercial property in this part of the state. We need to do more research, but it appears that he's made loans on a number of strip shopping centers, both of the new golf courses, and one of the resorts. We have a list of the properties from the fine print in the latest annual report. We'll need to find out exactly who owns them and what the loan terms are. He's also loaned money on at least twenty-five condos in the Miami, Florida area. Again, we need to know what they're worth and who owns them. We don't know if the amounts of the loans were appropriate or if someone was using the loans as a way to skim money from the fund. And we don't know if the loans are being repaid."

"We might find that these were good investments at the time, and that the recession has affected the fund and nothing more sinister has occurred," he continued. This remark was greeted with grunts and moans of disbelief. "I don't think so, either," Alex agreed. "I bet we'll find that these loans were all made to Wheeler and his crowd. Some of the loan proceeds were probably used legitimately, but I'll bet that a significant portion of the money can't be accounted for. And that these condos in Florida are taxpayer-subsidized vacation homes," he concluded.

"What 'research' do we need to do?" Sam asked. "If you want to know about the condition of the properties here and whether they're occupied or not, I can drive around and do that for you," he said. "I've probably done maintenance on most of them," he added. "If I know the tenants, I can ask questions and find out about the landlords," he offered. "I'll just need that list."

Beth leaned forward. "I desperately wanted to find that everything was in order. But the more I thought about the people involved, the more nervous I got. Wheeler was one of my students and he was always up to no good. With what I've heard tonight, I'm convinced we've got a big problem. My brother-in-law is Tim Knudsen. He's the realtor with signs all over town. He's got all the contacts we need to get the ownership and mortgage documents on these properties. And I know he's interested in this because we talked about it last week. If you approve, I'll ask him to get the information for us and I'll organize it all into an excel spreadsheet," she offered, proud to contribute.

"I was just going to suggest Tim," Sam said. "I do a lot of handyman work for him. He'll be discrete. We can assess the properties together, and get the info to you.

"Perfect," Tonya declared. "You know, after I talked to Maggie and Alex, I was feeling daunted by all of this. And now, I'm feeling like we've got the right team to get this thing turned around. I can't thank you all enough," she said steadily. "It may take some time to gather this information, but how about we all get together next Wednesday, same time, to see where we're at?"

Electronic and old-fashioned paper calendars were consulted and the consensus was that Wednesday nights were open and would be reserved for a standing meeting. "One last thing," Alex said and paused until all eyes were upon him. "We're looking at major corruption here. Felonies. Possibly mob connections. We need to be very cautious. Don't talk about what you're investigating or what you've found out, other than within this group. At least for now," he admonished.

The mood in the room was somber as John rushed in, with apologies for being late. "Looks like you're all done," he observed as people were rising and retrieving coats.

Alex asked Maggie to stay back so they could give John a summary of the meeting. Beth told them to keep the hummus. "I know John," she said. "He was probably too busy to eat lunch."

"Cat lovers are the best cooks," he teased. "I'm starved," he admitted. "I'd appreciate it. I'll drop the plate by your front door tomorrow."

John ate while Alex and Maggie filled him in on their research and conclusions. "Embezzlement from the general fund and probably from the pension fund, plus insider investments. We're turning over some big rocks, here," John observed. "I hope everyone knows to be careful and keep quiet," he said.

"We covered that very issue and everyone knows we're playing with fire," Alex assured him.

"So Sam and Tim will get us info on the pension fund investments, but how can we find out about the off-shore accounts implicated in the general fund transfers?" John asked.

"Unless our source at Town Hall can give us some additional documentation," Alex answered, "they'll have to turn it over voluntarily or we'll need to subpoena the Town. I'm researching how to do that," he said. "I'm doubtful that they'll cooperate voluntarily, no matter how much public pressure we put on them."

Alex yawned and looked at his watch. Maggie stood, saying that it was late and she needed to get home to feed Eve. John gathered up the now-empty serving dish and helped her on with her coat. When they reached Maggie's car, John held her door.

How long had it been since a man had opened her car door for her, Maggie wondered? Paul had abandoned this gallant gesture years ago. She murmured her thanks as she made a conscious effort to get into her seat as gracefully as possible.

"How about I pick you up at five-thirty on Saturday? Wear pants and clothes you can move in. Dress warm. It's supposed to be a clear day and we'll be outside for about an hour."

Maggie's emotions ran the gamut from elation that he had not forgotten about their date (is that what this was?) to terror that he had not forgotten (good Lord, was she going on a date after all of these years?). She returned his smile, hoping to hide the panic she felt and answered, in as casual a tone as she could muster, "Perfect. Will do. Thanks for the heads up. So – what do you have planned?"

He cocked one brow. "I thought you wanted more surprises in your life. How about we let this be one?" He was enjoying the bit of mystery he was creating. He continued kindly, "I remember you said you didn't know what you liked to do for fun. Well, one of the things we're going to do is something you used to be good at. I thought that would be a good place to start. Don't worry about a thing. We'll have fun. And if you don't like it, we'll do something else. How does that sound?" he assured her.

His manner and his very presence were a balm to her. His face was hidden in shadow but she sensed his concerned gaze. He's put a lot of thought into this, she realized with surprise. Maggie felt a sudden surge of tenderness toward him. "I'm sure it will be great fun and I can't wait," she replied. She couldn't be sure, but it looked like his step held more spring in it as he walked to his car.

Chapter 12

Sam pulled the list of pension fund properties from a folder as he turned out of the school parking lot at two forty-five on Thursday afternoon, grateful to get off work a few minutes early. Maggie was true to her word and didn't mind that he wouldn't finish painting her kitchen until Saturday. He and Tim were going to meet at seven after the realty office cleared out. He had time to do an assessment of three or four properties before then.

The afternoon was sunny, with high wispy clouds set in a vibrant blue sky. He loved driving on the curving roads he knew so well. He accelerated up a hill and around to the right as he approached a small strip center. He pulled in and parked in front of the Thai restaurant at the north end. In mid-afternoon, the restaurant was empty and the hostess sat on a stool by the door, listlessly swinging one foot while talking on her cell phone. She raised her head and nodded at Sam through the window as he passed by.

Only a handful of cars were in the lot at this time of day. Tenants consisted of a dry cleaner, a cell phone store, an optometrist, a beauty supply, and a physical therapy center. The therapist was the only one that was busy, with two cars arriving while he inspected the center's physical condition; parents dropping off school-aged kids getting therapy for sports injuries. The lot and buildings were in good shape, and even if business did not appear to be booming, all of the spaces were leased and open for business. Sam made notes on a pad of paper.

The next property was larger, with bigger stores. Two buildings on pads by the main entrance stood empty. One had been home to a movie rental store and the other had been a branch office of a major bank. Neither survived the recession. It appeared that the theme of this center was discount goods. It housed a used appliance retailer, a thrift shop benefitting the local hospital, a clothing consignment store that catered to the young and hip crowd, and the Forever Friends animal shelter. This center was busy. The clothing store was packed with high school kids, socializing more than shopping. Groups of teens were clustered by their cars in the parking lot.

The thrift store was empty and he recognized the volunteer behind the counter. Debra attended his church. "I didn't know you worked here," he said as he entered.

"I volunteer three afternoons a week," she told him. "I'm good at bargain hunting and thought they could use my help. I usually work in the back, sorting through the donations and pricing things. I also do the displays," she said proudly, sweeping her arm toward the store behind her. "I've arranged things by color. I got the idea from that home-goods store at the mall. Looks terrific there and I think it works even better here. Plus our prices are a fraction of what you pay there," she said. Before he could reply, she continued, "We're short-handed this week, so I've been working the register. It's been pretty steady all day. Only got quiet a few minutes ago."

Sam remembered that Debra was a non-stop talker and realized that this trait might be an advantage now. She launched into a tirade about the way the kids clogged up the lot after school, probably driving away their customers. When she paused to take a sip of her coffee, Sam asked, "Does your roof leak? I couldn't help but notice the stains on the ceiling."

Debra laughed, "You are a handyman through and through, aren't you? Yes, the roof leaks. Has the whole time we've been here. We pay exorbitant rent to some out-of-state landlord that never fixes anything. You don't get to talk to a person when you call. You can only leave a message. We've sent letters with our rent checks, but it does no good. Personally, I would break our lease and move out, but the hospital board won't even consider it. They say that the income is good enough and we don't want to stir up trouble by breaking our lease. It's an out-of-state landlord, for heaven's sake. What do we care? I don't see it myself," she said.

"The appliance store can't get their repairs made, either. I talk to those girls. They say the same thing, their management is afraid to rock the boat. Except at the consignment store. They get everything they want and the landlord doesn't make them stick to any of the rules about keeping the parking lot and sidewalks clean, or anything. I don't get that. Of all the tenants, they are the worst. Those kids drive around here like maniacs, leave fast food trash all over the lot, and intimidate the other shoppers. They even take the handicapped spots," she huffed as she peered over her half-moon spectacles at him. She lowered her voice and leaned in, "I suspect that some of them are selling drugs in that lot. I've seen how they do it on TV. I'd bet dollars to donuts that's what's going on," she confided.

Sam looked dutifully shocked and, privately, thought that she might be on to something. Before he could comment, she straightened and said, "You didn't come in here to chat with me. Are you looking for something in particular?"

Not a good spontaneous liar, Sam collected his thoughts as he cast his glance around the shop. He spotted a small ceramic vase and said that he wanted to surprise Joan with flowers and get her something new to put them in. He indicated the vase and Debra praised him for his good taste as she wrapped it carefully in newspaper and collected the three-dollar price. Sam made a mental note to buy Joan flowers as he headed to his truck.

Frank Haynes turned into the center, a malnourished lab secured in the large crate in his backseat. He was following the driveway around to the back entrance of Forever Friends when he spotted the older man with a slight limp walking purposefully to a truck at the far end of the lot. He's out of place, Haynes mused.

Haynes completed the intake paperwork quickly and skipped the one ritual that he truly enjoyed; spending time with the animals. The receptionist was surprised when Haynes shook his head and snapped that he didn't have time to take any of the dogs out to the exercise pen. This was a first, she thought, but based upon his brusque manner, she didn't comment.

Haynes snatched his keys off the counter and headed out the door without a backward glance. When he drove around to the front of the center, he was dismayed to see that the truck was still there and the occupant was intently watching the area in front of the consignment store. What the hell was he still doing here? He quickly pulled into a parking spot and awkwardly craned his neck to see what was so interesting.

Both men observed three boys and one girl surrounding an older male, probably in his late twenties, off to one side. Their heads were bent, looking at something the man was holding. They weren't laughing and jostling or engaging in the easy conversations of the other groups. Obviously a drug buy.

Goddamn those Delgado brothers, Haynes seethed. They never know when to stop. I was a fool to allow them into this. They knew the rules; no drugs, no prostitutes, no numbers running anywhere near the centers. Clean financial fraud they'd be able to cover up forever. That's why I agreed to those condos in Florida; they could run their girls and dope down there. Fucking white-trash, bottom-feeding petty thugs.

Haynes turned back to the truck at the far end of the lot. That nosey bastard is still there. He knows what's going on. I'll bet the other tenants do, too. Not to mention the high-school kids.

The man started up his truck and pulled out of the lot. Wheeler followed. The man's next two stops – both at centers that were part of their scheme – confirmed his worst fears. Someone was on to them. Haynes ground his teeth as he spun his car around and accelerated back to his office. No sense letting this bastard in the truck know he was being followed. He reached into the giant bottle of antacids that he kept in his console and popped a handful like they were M&Ms. Time to make sure that everything was in place to finger Wheeler. And that nothing could lead to himself.

Dr. John Allen was busy on that Thursday afternoon as well. He had a rare break between patients and decided to drive out to that venerable old restaurant and inn on the outskirts of town known as The Mill. Built in 1922 on the site of a nineteenth-century sawmill that harnessed power from the Shawnee River, nothing remained of the original structure except the old red bricks that had been reused when the inn was built and the wood from the millwheel that had been incorporated into the bar. The Mill had seen its ups and downs over the decades. When it opened, it housed a still and speakeasy. During the thirties a fire destroyed the structure and locals considered it a point of pride that patrons carried the bar out of the burning restaurant to the safety of the lawn and continued to drink while the rest burned to the ground. The restaurant and bar were rebuilt and The Mill left its wild adolescence behind and settled into middle age as a gracious retreat of comfort and hospitality.

In a bid to attract families and a younger crowd, The Mill operated an outdoor skating rink in the winter months. Weather was unpredictable and synthetic ice was now readily available and more dependable, so The Mill offered skating on its synthetic rink set on the banks of the Shawnee. It was this rink that drew John to The Mill that afternoon.

The restaurant was deserted except for an elderly couple lingering over coffee as John approached the hostess stand. A trim young woman in a conservative black dress and heels approached him with a smile. "Dr. Allen. I'm Katie McConnell. You take care of our cat, Felix. Lunch?" she asked. "We've closed the restaurant until dinner, but I'm sure we can serve you something in the bar," she offered.

"Not necessary," John said. "I've come to make reservations for dinner Saturday night and to see if the ice rink will still be open on Saturday. Your website said that you close it down the end of February, but I see that it's still there."

"We aren't planning on having it open. No one wants to skate in March anymore. I guess we're all too anxious for spring. The maintenance crew is taking it down on Monday," she said. She looked at John intently and could see that he was disappointed.

"Any chance I could pay for a couple of hours of exclusive use of the rink? Make it worth your while to keep it open for me?" he asked.

"You know," Katie said slowly, thinking. "I'm sure we could. How many people are you bringing?" she asked.

"Just me and my date," he said, and the words sounded both foreign and welcome to his ears. He continued, "She used to skate as a kid and I thought it would be fun. I played hockey when I was young but haven't been on skates for years. Hope I don't break a hip," he added.

"No. I'm sure you won't," Katie said reassuringly. "It's like riding a bike. You'll see."

John made the arrangements, thanked Katie, and whistled his way back to his car.

Sam waited in his truck across the street from New Way Realty until only Tim's car remained in the lot. He knocked on the locked back door at seven-fifteen and Tim immediately let him in. The two old friends were not in the mood for small talk. They both had information to share.

They headed to the break room to brew a fresh pot of coffee. Sam broke the ice by telling Tim he had driven around to several of the pension fund properties that afternoon and his conclusions were not comforting. Two of the centers were well maintained; two were not. Two of them were fully leased, the others were half vacant. He then recounted his conversation with Debra at the hospital thrift shop and his observation of a suspected drug deal in the parking lot.

Tim listened thoughtfully. "This ties in to what I found," he said. The two men took the pot of coffee to a conference room. Tim slid a stack of papers over to Sam. "I've printed out all of the ownership records for the properties that the pension fund has loans on. I've printed out the loan documents, too," he added. "They fall into two different groups. One set of properties is owned by Wheeler or his cronies. The other properties are owned by people I've known for years who try to make their living as decent landlords. I gave copies to Beth and she's going to put it all in her spreadsheet tonight. I thought we could drive around and look at the properties together. You could determine their condition and I could come up with a rough guess as to their value."

Sam agreed. "Let's look at the documents on the centers I went to this afternoon. I'll bet we'll find that the well maintained ones are owned by the Wheeler bunch and the struggling centers are owned by the honest landlords."

"I'm guessing Wheeler has big loans with low payments and below-market interest rates. And the other loans have adjustable rates and huge payments that are crushing the honest landlords. They may be driving the honest ones out of business and buying their distressed properties for a song at foreclosure, without anyone suspecting that they are part of a conspiracy to drive them out of business. The more we look into this, the worse it gets," Tim observed.

"Pretty clever plan they had going," Sam said. "Don't they call it predatory lending? If they hadn't done so much of it and jeopardized payments to pensioners, we would never have investigated."

"Yep – that's what happens when you get greedy," Tim nodded. "And this group is really greedy."

Chuck Delgado was nervously pacing in his upstairs office while Russell Isaac wearily scanned a discarded copy of the mornings' sports section.

"Jesus, Chuck. I'm too old for this two a.m., clandestine-meeting shit. Why the hell couldn't we have met with him earlier? Next time, grow some balls when he calls."

"Why don't I just let you clean up this mess? Jackass."

"Your brother is the genius who was keeping the tab. He wasn't supposed to let us run short of money. Didn't you guys have this all set up with guaranteed annuities or some shit like that?"

"We didn't create this recession. We're not the only ones got hit. Everybody in the market got hit. If it hadn't ..." Delgado broke off at the sound of the sharp series of knocks on the door downstairs.

"He's here. Just shut the fuck up and let me do the talking," Delgado hissed as he buzzed Haynes in.

Haynes sprinted up the stairs without a trace of fatigue. Both men stood as he entered the room. Delgado began, "We're getting this all worked out, Frank. Ron's got a plan. It'll just take some time."

Haynes cut him off. "Time is what I'm afraid we don't have. You know that bitch Holmes held a meeting at the Library and formed a committee to investigate."

"Bunch of brainless do-gooders, Frank," Delgado interrupted. "They won't be able to trace this. Probably spend most of their time talking about their kids and swapping recipes. Like my wife's book club. Women don't focus on shit like this."

"You're a moron – you're both morons. They've got that new woman in town on their committee. She's a forensic accountant. And they've got Alex Scanlon, too."

"That prick?" Delgado exploded. I thought we were done with him when he left the prosecutor's office and set up his law firm.

"Nope. He's back," Haynes assured them.

"No matter who's on their committee," Isaac interjected, "they'll have a hell of a time unraveling all of this. We'll have the money back in there shortly. And they won't be able to trace it."

"Yeah, Frank, relax. Leave this to us," Delgado added.

"I don't think so, boys. Not this time," Haynes deliberately drew out what he came to tell them. "I went for a drive this afternoon." He paused to let their discomfort intensify.

"Christ, Frank, it's the middle of the night here. What did you see?"

"That janitor from the school was driving around this afternoon, canvasing the centers. Watched a drug deal in front of the clothing exchange. I'm sure he knew what he was looking at."

"Oh, for God's sake, Frank. Is that all? Some handyman driving around? He must've been looking for work."

"Sitting in his truck watching the kids in front of the exchange?"

"Probably talking on his cell phone."

"He wasn't on the phone. I followed him to two of our other centers before I turned away. I didn't want him to suspect he was being followed."

Isaac glanced nervously at Delgado. "Frank's right, Chuck. This can't be a coincidence. They're a lot closer to us than we thought. You and Ron need to accelerate your plan to get us out of this."

Delgado sat heavily into his desk chair. "Alright. We'll do what needs to be done here. You don't need to worry. I'm on it."

"Don't fuck this up any further, Chuck," Haynes replied. "We don't want you doing anything stupid. We just need this to quietly blow over." Haynes nodded to Isaac and turned toward the stairs.

"Frank's right," Isaac said to Delgado before snatching his jacket from the back of a chair. "This is bad."

Delgado dismissed Isaac with a crude gesture and picked up his cell phone. He scrolled to his brother's number and texted "Cousin in hospital" – their code that they needed to meet immediately. He knew that Ron was an early riser and would get the message as soon as he got up. No sense going home for only a few hours. Besides, his wife was used to his staying out all night. Probably preferred it, the ungrateful broad.

He dozed fitfully on the familiar leather sofa in his office and was startled awake when his office door creaked open and his brother stepped across the threshold. He sat up groggily and rubbed a hand over his balding scalp. "Jesus, Ron. It's still dark out. What the hell time do you get up?"

"It's five-fifteen. I'm on my way to the gym. This is my normal time. Lots of people are up and out this early. Maybe you'd like to come with me sometime? Give it a try?" he said, staring pointedly at his brother's protruding paunch.

"I didn't call you here for you to give me shit because I'm fat," Chuck retorted. "Haynes came to see me last night. That committee formed by Tonya Holmes may be on to us."

"What? No way. This is too complicated. The Feds would have trouble putting it together. How in the hell could a bunch of witless citizens figure it out? He must be wrong."

"Haynes tailed one of them, investigating our centers. I think we take care of him. Send a message to the rest of them."

"Hold on. If we need to send a message, we want to make sure we have the right target. Who did Haynes follow?"

"Some school janitor who does handyman work on the side."

"He doesn't sound like a threat. He can't be the brains of their committee. Who else is on it?

"An old teacher, the vet, that new woman at Rosemont — Haynes says she is a forensic accountant. She could definitely be trouble. And Alex Scanlon."

"He's your target. He's got plenty of contacts at the prosecutor's office, and I'll bet he's still got political ambitions."

"Plus he's a queer," Chuck volunteered.

"Something to distract him. Take his attention away from all of this. Nothing more. We don't want to shine a bright light on all of this. That would be the worst possible outcome. So rein your boys in." Ron Delgado held up a hand to silence his brother. "I don't want to know any more about it. Just do what you have to do. And don't tell me about it."

Chuck Delgado sneered at his brother. "You've always been too good to get your hands dirty. Leave it to Chuck. And now you try to tell me how to do it? Get the fuck out of my office. I'll handle this."

"Chuck. That's not what I meant," Ron attempted to placate his brother.

"I mean it. Get the fuck out."

Ron Delgado abandoned any further attempt to placate his brother and headed back to his car. If he really hustled, he wouldn't be more than a few minutes late for his appointment with his trainer.

Chapter 13

Maggie woke before dawn on Saturday morning. She tore back the covers, excited to begin unpacking and settling into Rosemont. The movers had delivered her things the afternoon before, four days ahead of schedule. Sam arrived shortly before seven to finish painting her kitchen. She fed Eve, grabbed her coffee, and decided to get her closet in order. She was feeling excited and terrified, in equal measure, over the prospect of her date with John. She had no idea what to wear and needed to root through her things anyway.

By the time she finished, she had tried on half a dozen sweaters and selected a sapphire-blue cashmere that showed off her eyes. She relegated four sweaters to the donation bag, along with various slacks and shirts that no longer fit or that she never wore. Cleaning house, improving her feng shui, making room for new things, she told herself.

Maggie stood back and surveyed with satisfaction the neatly arranged clothes and shoes. The matching hangers, shoeboxes and bins that she bought at the organizer store made everything look neat and tidy. Rather like a picture from the store's catalog, she thought proudly. She snapped a photo on her cell phone and sent it to Susan, who was a compulsive organizer. She'll be very proud of me, Maggie thought.

She stretched and checked the time, and was shocked to see that it was almost noon. The day was gloriously sunny with a hint of spring in the air. She and Eve could use some exercise. She was also hungry and the kitchen was definitely off limits, so she snapped the leash on Eve and they headed toward Pete's. She decided to take the long way there so she could explore the other side of the Town Square. Eve trotted happily at her heels as she passed a nail salon, a combination tailor and shoe repair shop, a copy/fax/printer center, and a real estate office.

Maggie crossed the street and turned the corner. The shops on this side of the Square were more upscale and retail-oriented. On the corner was a tiny old-fashioned candy store with ropes of colorful silk flowers (now a bit faded, but still pretty) framing a small window filled with charming fabric-covered boxes of candy tied with large satin bows. Inside was crowded with cases full of trays of chocolates; truffles and crèmes and candies molded into shapes of rabbits, dogs, cats, frogs, and more. The alluring aroma of chocolate seeped out onto the sidewalk.

A jeweler was next, flanked by a gift shop with an inviting window decorated for spring with porcelain rabbits, woven baskets in pastels decorated with ribbons and flowers, and colorful china and tableware. Maggie made a mental note to come back to explore "Celebrations', as the shop was called. Maybe she would invite a group for Easter dinner, and do her dining room table up with those porcelain rabbits running down the center. She slowly walked away from the window, glancing back over her shoulder and contemplating the possibilities for her Easter table.

Her mind was running through a guest list and menu when she arrived at Pete's. The shops had been busy and the sidewalks crowded, and Pete's was packed. Eve held court, graciously accepting pats and ear rubs from other patrons, as Maggie ordered a spinach salad with chicken to go. While her order was being prepared, Maggie went through to Laura's and picked up a loaf of multi-grain bread and some strawberry croissants for breakfast. Laura was quiet and distracted behind the counter, murmuring only a brief hello to Maggie as she bagged her purchases and handed Maggie her change.

"Are you alright?" Maggie asked. She looked at Laura closely and realized, with a bit of alarm, that she looked thinner than before and very pale.

Laura looked from side to side and leaned in to Maggie as she whispered, "You're the only one who's noticed. We weren't going to say anything just yet. I'm pregnant. Only seven weeks along. And sick as a dog," she confided.

"That's wonderful!" Maggie cried, and then quickly lowered her voice. "You poor thing. Hopefully, you'll feel better at the end of the first trimester."

"That's what I'm praying. Working around food is torture. But at least I have my morning sickness in the evening, which is a good thing for a baker," she added.

Maggie squeezed her hand, assured her she would keep their secret, and went back to Pete's to collect her lunch and head home.

At four o'clock on Saturday afternoon, Alex and his partner Marc arrived at the service entrance of Pete's to set up for the evening's performance. This would be Marc's first gig since the skiing accident where he broke his collarbone and right arm. He had worked hard in physical therapy to regain his strength and flexibility. And he had practiced incessantly to recover his timing and stamina.

"You're here early," Pete said as he hurried across the restaurant to help them carry in the keyboard and sound equipment. "You're not on until eight o'clock."

"I know," Marc said. "I'm just nervous. Wanted to test out the equipment before you get busy. Make sure I still know how to set everything up."

"He was pacing around the house and driving me crazy," Alex told Pete. "So I suggested we load up and come over here."

"You'll be fine," Pete assured Marc. "Like riding a bike. And everyone misses you. I'm expecting a full house. I've had a sign up all week that you'll be back tonight. People have been calling to confirm. You were always one of my biggest draws," he said as he patted Marc on the back.

"That's good to hear, I guess. I'm not sure if I'll live up to my reputation, though."

"Of course you will. I've been listening to you at home and you're better than ever. A full house is exactly what you need," Alex said.

"And you should eat something because I know the crowd is going to keep you going for a long time. Tonight's special is good.

Let me bring it to you," Pete said as he ushered Alex and Marc to seats at the bar.

Maggie was finally ready at four forty-five. She started at two, thinking she would have time to answer her emails when she was dressed. Instead, she spent the entire time changing outfits and tweaking her hair and makeup. Eve lay close at hand on the rug in Maggie's bedroom, head down on her outstretched paws, eyes focused intently on her master. Maggie asked her opinion on various outfits, and Eve either raised one eyebrow or cautiously wagged her tail. She's handling me like I handle Susan, Maggie thought. Afraid to give an opinion in case she disapproves of the outfit I like best. Intuitive creature, Maggie thought. In the end, Maggie settled on the original sapphire-blue cashmere, a nicely cut pair of jeans, heeled boots, and her leather jacket.

She headed downstairs and into the kitchen as Sam was touching up a spot on the far wall. "Wow!" she exclaimed. "It looks absolutely fabulous! Amazing what a fresh coat of paint will do. This color brings out the warm tones of the cabinets. And you've done a terrific job."

Sam carefully finished and turned to face Maggie. "It's my turn to say 'Wow!' You're all dressed up and looking sharp. Are you going out?"

Maggie blushed, and was furious with herself for doing so. "Yes. And thank you. I'm having dinner with John Allen. But it's not a date or anything. Just a quick dinner. To discuss committee business."

A smile spread across Sam's face as she spoke. "I've known John for more than forty years. He's one of the finest men I've ever met. If it was a date, I'd think that would be a really good thing for both of you."

"I'm not sure I'm ready for all of that yet. Or that I'll ever be ready. I've got enough changes in my life right now," she said dismissively.

Sam held her eyes with his steady gaze. "So what's one more? Are you getting any younger? Why postpone something that might bring you a lot of happiness. If God puts something good in your path, I say you should grab it. Just stay open to the possibility, OK?"

Maggie nodded and murmured that she would do that, mostly to shut him up and change the subject as she was becoming increasingly nervous with all of this serious talk about dating. This was going to be dinner. Period. She'd be home, watching TV with Eve, by nine-thirty.

Chapter 14

John Allen pulled up a few minutes early. Maggie fumbled with the cantankerous lock on the heavy front door. Her hands were clammy and she felt faintly queasy. Eve was yipping and jumping, and shot out onto the porch the minute the door was open wide enough to let her through.

"Quite the welcoming committee," he said as he scooped up Eve.

"Her manners need improving, that's for sure. I'm sorry," Maggie said as John stepped over the threshold and deposited the squirming creature securely inside. "I've never trained a dog before. We need to sign up for obedience lessons."

"There's lots of options for that. Group classes and private trainers. I'll email you a list."

John helped her into her jacket and she picked up her purse from the foyer table. In a voice that she hoped sounded casual, she asked, "So – are you ready to reveal where we're headed? Or is it still top secret?"

John held the door of his Suburban open for her. "Partially. We're going to The Mill for dinner. Have you heard of it?"

"I've seen their ad in the paper. I understand it's been around for ages; has quite a colorful history," Maggie replied. "I thought I'd take my kids there when they visit. I'd like them to see the countryside around here. Southern California has trees, but not Hansel-and-Gretel woods like these. I can't take my eyes off of the scenery."

"I've lived in the Midwest all my life, and I can't take my eyes off of it, either. But we don't have any of your California beaches," he added as they set off. "Nothing beats a walk on the beach." They kept up amiable small talk along the way and her jittery nerves were beginning to calm as he turned the Suburban off of the main road and onto the driveway for The Mill. He parked and sprang out of the car to open her door. Instead of climbing the stairs to the main entrance, John led them around the side of the building to a skating rink, now deserted, set up under strings of fairy lights. The blazing colors of the sunset were reflected in the nearby river. The air was crisp and the scene was serene.

"What a perfect spot for skating!" Maggie exclaimed. "I'm definitely going to bring my granddaughters here when they visit during winter. I can teach them how to skate. This will be fabulous," she enthused.

"I was hoping you'd like it," John said, obviously pleased with her reaction. "You told me you figure-skated as a kid. You won some competitions. And that you don't remember what you like to do for fun. So I thought this might be a good place to start," he continued. "It's been a long time since I've been on skates. I hope I can keep up with you. The skate rental is inside. Let's go get suited up."

Maggie turned to him with a mixture of amazement and trepidation. "We're going to skate? You get high marks for originality," she laughed. "I'm not sure you won't be taking me out of here on a stretcher," she added as she raced up the stairs ahead of him.

It took about ten minutes for John to rustle up someone with a key to the cabinet holding the rental skates, but they finally managed to find the appropriate sizes and get themselves laced in, with their shoes parked together companionably under a bench at the side of the rink. Night had fallen and the black ice shone in the reflected fairy lights.

John stepped on the ice first and offered Maggie his hand. They both wobbled a bit, but soon found their footing and began gliding around the rink. They fell into a steady rhythm and Maggie took John's arm. "OK, Dr. Allen," she said. "It's obvious that this rink wasn't supposed to be open for business tonight. The sign by the skate rental said it closed last weekend. So how did you make this happen?"

"It was nothing, really. I came out here on Thursday and they were happy to do it," he said making light of his efforts. "You're good," he observed. "Actually, we're both pretty good. Having fun?"

"More fun than I've had in I-can't-remember-when," she said. "This is magic. I'd forgotten how wonderful it feels to glide along with the cold breeze blowing through your hair. Thank you for going to all of the trouble."

"This is a very special evening," he replied simply.

Maggie attempted a scratch spin and made herself dizzy; spotting was something she'd have to practice. John helped her off the ice to the bench, where she sat motionless until she regained her equilibrium. Her checks were red, her nose runny and her carefully styled hair was blown to bits. But her eyes sparkled and her smile was joyful and genuine. John thought she looked incredible.

They sat for a moment longer, exhilarated by the knowledge that they could still skate. It was, after all, like riding a bike. John stood and they climbed the stairs to the dining room. She stopped at the Ladies Room to check herself in the mirror and was sorry she had. Her hair and makeup were beyond repair, but she was having such fun she didn't much care.

They were shown to a cozy table in the corner by the windows overlooking the now-empty rink and the river. The menu was extensive and Maggie realized she was famished. John asked her to select an appetizer and she ordered the garlic chicken flatbread. She had a glass of wine and he had a beer. They both ordered the chef's special salmon with polenta and cucumber beet salsa.

Conversation flowed easily over their leisurely meal. "We've talked mostly about me," Maggie said. "Which is really bad manners on my part. I'd like to know about you. Tell me the John Allen story."

He warmed to her interest and talked at length about what had evidently been a very happy childhood. His dad was a dairy farmer and his mom a hard-working farm wife. She also gave piano lessons. Both passed away years ago and the farm sold to make way for a subdivision. He played football and hockey in high school and was still an avid fan. Preferred college sports to the pros, but watched it all in his free time. Loved working with animals as a kid, but witnessed the hardness of his dad's life and knew he didn't want to be a farmer. So he decided to become a vet. He loved his job and his patients. The business aspect of running his practice was not his strong suit, but after an office manager embezzled from him years ago, he accepted that he had to attend to this detail.

"That must have been awful," Maggie stated. "It happens more often than you might think," and resisted the urge to unburden herself about Paul's embezzlement. Not yet, she told herself. Before John could ask her about her remark, she continued "You haven't told me if you've ever been married or have kids," she said.

"I was married for fourteen years. We divorced fifteen years ago. Never had children. Which I regretted. I always wanted to be a dad," he stated matter-of-factly. Maggie looked into his face and waited for him to continue. "Sharon was fun and vivacious when we got married. My parents thought that she was shallow and selfish and never liked her. I was charmed by her. I was a serious bookworm and was flattered that this popular, fun-loving spirit chose me. Turns out my parents were right," he said with a rueful smile. "She never grew out of her self-centered ways and constantly used me and everyone else in her life. She got so that she couldn't hold a job; couldn't get along with her co-workers. Nothing was ever enough. Even though we had agreed to have kids, she never wanted to ruin her body with a pregnancy. She was totally selfish," he concluded.

"Did you finally have enough and end it?" Maggie couldn't help asking. "I know what it's like to be married to an egocentric. Paul always made sure he was the center of attention. It gets old after a while."

"I found out that she was having an affair. I suspect it wasn't the first. I always worked long hours and wasn't around to constantly entertain her. And she wasn't good at entertaining herself. So that was it for me. I filed for divorce, offered her a fair settlement, and she was on her way. She moved to Chicago and I heard that she died there three years ago," he finished.

"Being cheated on is a bitter pill to swallow. I think Paul was having an affair when he died. It haunts me. One day I'll find out." She couldn't believe she was being so open with him. "You would have been a wonderful father," she stated. "You haven't wanted to remarry?"

"I'd like to. I believe in marriage. Just haven't found the right gal. And believe me, I've looked," he said. "Dating services, online, blind dates arranged by friends. I'm not going to get myself into another bad marriage. I'm happy on my own until I meet the right person. And it looks like we need some dessert," he said, changing the serious mood and waving the waiter over to take their order.

Maggie and John were the last diners to leave the restaurant. A full moon illuminated the clouds and the Courthouse was incandescent against the surrounding trees. The Square was deserted with the notable exception of Pete's. Cars filled every available parking spot. The door was propped open and the crowd spilled out onto the sidewalk. They could hear someone playing jazz piano.

"I forgot," John turned to Maggie. "Marc is playing tonight. Alex's partner? He's one of my favorites. He always packs 'em in at Pete's. Would you like to stop in?"

"I haven't been out this late in months," she laughed. "I can't believe I'm not dead on my feet. And you're the one who worked all day. If you aren't too tired, I'd love to." John pulled to the curb on the other side of the Square and took Maggie's hand as they walked back to Pete's.

Inside, the restaurant was dimly lit and buzzing with energy. Pete wound them through the crowd to a table by the back door. Marc was in the middle of a set.

They had just settled into their seats and ordered coffee when the piercing sound of a fire truck could be heard above the din, approaching fast. It was barely starting to recede when another siren could be heard in the distance, then another. Several people stepped outside to see where the trucks were headed.

Marc continued to play, unaware of the disturbance. John and Maggie, wedged in the back, stayed put and watched the swell of people by the front door. Maggie thought she recognized Pete, talking to a man who was clearly agitated. The man tore off into the night as Pete quickly skirted the room and knelt by their table. He leaned in to be heard above the noise.

"Alex's law practice is on fire," he said simply. "And his home." Pete paused to let the implications of this coincidence sink in. John and Maggie got quickly to their feet, snatched their coats from the vacant chair and followed Pete out the back door.

"Alex is on the way to his office now," Pete said. "I'm going to tell Marc and close down the bar as soon as I can get everyone out. Would you take Marc to their house? I'll come as soon as I can."

"Of course," John said. "Go. I'll bring my car back here. Send him out the back door." John turned to Maggie. "I'll run you home now, if that's OK," he said.

"No way," Maggie replied. "I'm going with you. All hands on deck, I think." They retrieved John's car and waited in silence until a frantic Marc burst through the back door.

Chapter 15

Two police cars blocked the entrance to the street. A plume of dark smoke snaked up into the cloudy night sky. John pulled to the curb and the acrid smell of burning wood engulfed them. Marc leapt out of the car before it came to a stop and raced toward his house. John followed, with Maggie bringing up the rear. A police officer intercepted Marc in the driveway.

"You'll have to stay back, sir," he told Marc firmly, spreading his arms to block Marc's progress.

"This is my house," Marc choked as he struggled to get past the officer.

"Was anyone at home? Any pets?"

"No, we were both out, and we don't have pets."

"The fire captain wants to speak to you. I'll tell him who you are. In the meantime, wait over there with your neighbors. They've been very concerned about you," he said, pointing to the small group huddled together on the front lawn of the house next door.

John took his arm and steered him to the group indicated by the officer. A matronly-looking woman in a wooly bathrobe stepped forward and wrapped her arms around Marc. "We were so worried," she cried. "Is Alex with you?" she asked, looking over Marc's shoulder at John.

"No," John answered. "He's at his office. There's a fire there too," he stated. "Marc was playing at Pete's. That's where we all were when the fires broke out. Alex went to his office and we brought Marc here."

The neighbor drew in a sharp breath. "Two fires at once? Then this was intentional. We've been talking. We thought it might be." She released a dazed Marc. "I'm so relieved you're both alright." Marc nodded and silently stepped away to watch the sure and steady destruction before him.

"Why did you suspect the fire was set intentionally?" John asked.

"I was in my kitchen. I heard a big bang from this direction. I ran to my door and looked out. I can see my back yard and part of theirs," she explained, pointing toward the burning house. "I saw two men scrambling over their back fence. My husband heard it from our bedroom. He went out the front door." She turned to a man who had joined them while she was talking. "Tell them," she said.

"The explosion was really loud. I knew it was close. I went out the front door and smelled gasoline. The house was engulfed in flame," he continued. He pointed to his wife. "She came to the door and I yelled for her to call 911. All hell broke loose around here then. Everyone on the street heard the explosion. People were running up here. Several of us tried to get near the house to see if they were home, but the heat was overpowering," he said. "We were around back, trying to find a way to get in when the firefighters arrived. They got us out of there in a hurry."

"They must think it's arson," a nearby man chimed in. "The police arrived shortly after the firefighters got here. They've been questioning all of us."

"Did anyone see anything else?" Maggie asked.

"I don't think so," the man said.

A new set of headlights down the street signaled Alex's arrival. As Marc had done only minutes before, Alex ran toward the chaos. John started toward him and Maggie grabbed his arm. "No. Give them a moment alone with this," she said softly. Alex slowed his pace and came to stand, shoulder to shoulder with Marc, watching the material trappings of their lives disintegrate. Marc lifted his arm to Alex's shoulder, and both men straightened and stood a little taller.

A firefighter told the neighbors that the fire was out and to contact the police if anyone remembered anything else. Reluctant to leave but with nothing left to do, they murmured their goodnights and headed to their homes and uneasy beds.

John and Maggie approached Alex and Marc. The woman next door joined them and asked if they would like to stay with her for a few days.

"That's very kind of you," Marc said. "We haven't even thought of that yet."

"I couldn't sleep right now," Alex added. "You go back to bed. We'll talk to you tomorrow. And thank you," he said, as he gave her shoulder a squeeze and she headed off to her house.

They stood on the now-deserted lawn and watched silently as the firefighters packed up their equipment and prepared to leave. A police officer advised them that he would remain on guard until the property was fenced off.

"Nothing's going to happen tonight," the officer said. "Go get some rest. You're going to have a busy day tomorrow."

Alex and Marc were again shaking their heads "no" when Maggie took charge. "You two are coming home with me," she announced. "I obviously have plenty of room. You can sleep or stay up for the rest of the night and you won't bother me a bit. And you can remain with me as long as you like. Your insurance company will pay for a hotel, but you'll be more comfortable at Rosemont," she concluded.

Pete joined the group as Maggie was finishing. "That's a terrific idea," he agreed. "We can talk more there," he said as he took Alex's arm and steered him reluctantly down the driveway and back to his car.

Maggie and John lead the caravan back to Rosemont. She left John in charge of corralling Eve and ushering Pete, Marc and Alex into the house while she started a pot of coffee. The four men joined her in the kitchen as she set out mugs, cream and sugar.

Alex had been explaining what he found at his office. He slumped onto a stool at the kitchen island and turned to Maggie. "They suspect arson there, too," he told her. "Fortunately, my building is equipped with sprinklers. The firefighters got there right away and put the fire out quickly. We're a paperless office and we back up our systems every night, so we'll be able to function from temporary quarters on Monday. Our furniture is all badly damaged, but it was insured. We didn't lose anything that we can't easily replace," he concluded.

"You can use my upstairs room to see clients and hold meetings," Pete offered. "It's private and convenient. Heck – it might even bring in customers for me," he joked. "Schedule your appointments around meal times, OK?"

"Thanks," Alex replied with an attempt at a smile. "I'll think about it. I don't want to do anything that would make you a target, too."

Marc paced restlessly. "Who would do this to us?"

John uncrossed his arms and reached for the coffee pot. "It could be a hate crime," he said. "There are some deeply bigoted folks around here. You could be targeted for your lifestyle. Or it could be related to our investigation into the corruption at Town Hall."

Pete whistled softly. "I wondered if you were going to stir up a hornet's nest with that," he said. "What have you found out?"

Alex rubbed his hand wearily over his eyes. "Reader's Digest version – the pension fund has been making fraudulent loans on shopping centers owned by off-shore entities. The people managing the fund don't want the loans to be repaid. They want the properties to go into foreclosure. When they do, the pension fund takes a big loss and a different off-shore entity buys the property at the foreclosure sale for pennies on the dollar."

"Maybe I'm just slow here, but I don't get it," Marc stopped and turned toward the others.

"They got big loans on the shopping centers using inflated appraisals and pocketed most of the loan proceeds. Just like the cash-out refis that have been such a problem for the housing industry. They signed up tenants to look legitimate and then jacked up their rents with add-on charges that were buried in the fine print of the leases. All of the tenants in these centers are mom-and-pop businesses. They probably never had a lawyer look at their lease before they signed it." Maggie explained. Alex nodded in agreement.

She continued, "The rent they collect is just gravy. What they really want is for the property to go into foreclosure so they can buy it back cheaply. This appears to be a clever scheme to embezzle money from the pension fund in a way that appears legitimate. If the economy had not taken such a hit and the fund's other investments had continued to support the payments to pensioners, no one would have ever known," she concluded.

"Holy shit," Pete said. "Those fucking bastards – sorry Maggie."

"No – you've got that right," Maggie agreed.

"How big is this? Who exactly is part of it?" Pete asked.

"Not sure yet," Alex sighed. "We're just uncovering all of this. We think that it's all related to Wheeler and other Council Members."

"Except Tonya Holmes. And maybe Frank Haynes," John added. "The committee hasn't even met yet to go over all of this. We've been discrete. If this attack on you, Alex, is related to our investigation, I wonder what they know about it."

"Sam and Tim Knudsen drove around to inspect some of the centers. Maybe someone noticed them. That's the only thing I can think of," Alex replied.

"Unless someone is leaking information to them," Maggie said. "Or unless they have someone bugged. Now I'm sounding paranoid," she said sheepishly. "I must be watching too much TV."

"No," John said. "I was thinking the same thing. We need to be very careful here. People in high places will lose their jobs and may go to jail. They could have done this," he warned.

"When do you plan to go to the police?" Pete asked. "This is scary stuff."

"I guess we should get the committee together in the morning to figure out what to do now," Maggie replied. "And Pete – no one thinks you're involved with this and we should keep it that way. You and Laura have enough on your plates," she said, with a knowing look.

"Maybe the police will come up with something. Maybe whoever set the fires left clues behind," Marc said.

"The arson investigators from the insurance company may also be helpful," Maggie continued. "We've got lots of questions that we can't answer right now. We know that evil is afoot. The main thing is that no one was hurt."

"Absolutely right," John interjected. "Whoever did this knew you weren't going to be home. They didn't want to injure you. At least that's something." He checked his watch. "It's two-thirty in the morning. Tomorrow will be a busy day. We need to get some sleep," he said as he began gathering up coffee cups.

"Leave all of that," Maggie said. "I'll take care of it. You're right. I'll email Tonya tonight and ask her to call me first thing. Why don't we try to meet with the committee here sometime tomorrow? I'll coordinate all of that."

"Marc and I will want to go to the house in the morning to see if we can salvage anything," Alex said. Marc nodded his agreement.

"I'll pick you up and take you over there," John offered. "At eight. It'll be light then. You should try to get some sleep now."

"I'll feed you all breakfast first," Maggie said as she ushered the group out of her kitchen and turned out the light. Pete and John headed for the front door as Maggie lead Alex and Marc upstairs to the bedroom at the top of the stairs. "I think you'll be comfortable here," she said as she turned down the bed. "You can leave the TV on all night, if you like. I won't hear a thing in my room. I know you're keyed up, but at least lie down and rest. There is absolutely nothing you can do right now." With that, she gave them each a hug and closed the door behind her.

Maggie walked wearily down the stairs to collect Eve. She was surprised to see John waiting for her in the foyer.

"I wanted to make sure you got all locked up," he said.

Maggie smiled. "I'm careful," she assured him. "What a night," she sighed. "And we've got a big day ahead of us tomorrow."

John turned toward Maggie. She wondered if he was going to kiss her. She hoped he was going to kiss her. He hesitated, one hand on the door handle. She smiled up at him.

"Skating is still fun for me," Maggie said. "Thank you for reminding me."

John drew a slow breath and regarded her thoughtfully. Not now, he thought. Not with all of this distraction; with Alex and Marc at the top of the stairs. When I kiss this woman for the first time, I intend to rock her world. It was his turn to smile. He told her he enjoyed the evening and would see her in the morning. He opened the door and was gone.

Chapter 16

Tonya Holmes rose early on Sunday mornings. She relished the quiet time with her coffee and the Sunday paper before she and her husband sprang into action, getting their three school-aged children up and ready for church. They loved their church family and between Sunday school, the worship service, and fellowship time afterwards, Sunday morning was consumed with this ritual. The kids all had friends that they only saw at church and once they were out of bed, were excited about going. She retrieved her cell phone from her desk as she headed downstairs and saw her message light flashing. "It's Sunday morning, for heaven's sake. Whoever needs me can wait," she grumbled.

She set the phone on the kitchen counter while she made a pot of strong coffee and retrieved the paper. The incessant red light finally got the better of her and she checked her messages. She was alarmed to see an email from Maggie at almost three a.m. and was shocked at the terse message: "Fires destroyed Alex's home and office. Suspected arson. He and Marc are staying with me. John is picking them up at 8 a.m. to retrieve anything worth saving. May be related to our investigation. The committee needs to meet. Please call me. Be careful. Maggie."

Tonya checked the time – six o'clock. Too early to call someone who was still up at three. She flipped the paper open to search for any mention of the fires. On the bottom of page four, section B, was a tiny article noting that fires had broken out simultaneously at the home and the office of local attorney Alex Scanlon. No causes for the fires were known, it reported. "No church for me this morning," she sighed. Tonya tossed the paper onto the counter, filled two mugs with coffee, and climbed the stairs to wake her husband and fill him in on her plan.

Maggie had collapsed into bed as soon as she finished her email to Tonya. She faintly heard the TV in the room down the hall. Eve was conflicted over whether she should guard Maggie from the intruders or simply curl up and go to sleep. Sleep won over and Eve hopped up to her usual spot at Maggie's feet, circled, and settled down.

Maggie was awakened by Eve as it was just beginning to get light. For a moment, Maggie's only thought was that she was way too tired to get up. Then the memories of all that transpired the night before flooded back, bringing Maggie to her feet, fully alert and ready to start the day. She threw on an old pair of jeans and a sweatshirt and headed downstairs. The grandfather clock on the landing told her it was seven-thirty. John would be here soon to pick up Alex and Marc. John, she thought warmly. She would have to get back upstairs to run a comb through her hair, brush her teeth and slap on some blush.

Maggie let Eve out, picked up her paper and started the coffee. She checked her email and saw that Tonya had read her message. She fed Eve and raced upstairs to make herself more presentable. She was back down in the kitchen, chopping ham and green onions for omelets, when she heard John's car on her driveway. She let him in before he could ring the bell. She ushered him into the kitchen and they were softly talking when Alex came downstairs.

"Help yourself to coffee," Maggie said, pointing to the mugs on the counter. "Did you get any sleep?"

"Some," Alex said. "I kept waking up and seeing my office in flames. I kept thinking about who would do this to us. And thinking about how I can take care of my clients."

"You'll have a lot to do the next few weeks," John said. "One step at a time. Taking action will be the best medicine. You'll get through and beyond all of this. You'll see. I know it sounds trite, and easy for me to say, but you only lost stuff. Nothing that can't be replaced."

"John is absolutely right," Maggie agreed. "You'll start in today and will feel better about things tonight. Just don't look too far ahead; don't let yourself get overwhelmed by all that you have to do. It doesn't have to be done in one day. And you've got friends to help you," she said. "Now, the first step is to eat breakfast." She slid a fluffy omelet onto a plate with one of the strawberry croissants she purchased from Laura. "Enjoy. You've got to eat," she told Alex firmly, as Marc entered the kitchen.

"Wow, something smells good," Marc said as he gave Maggie a tired smile.

"You can be off as soon as you eat something." Maggie was pouring eggs into the pan when Eve began to bark and the doorbell rang. John answered the door and soon returned, preceded by Tonya.

"I'm so glad that I caught you before you all left," she said. "I'm devastated by what happened to you, but so thankful that you weren't hurt. I've already been on the phone with the Chief of Police and the Fire Marshall. They're all over this. They're competent and thorough. And they aren't connected to the Mayor or anyone on the Council. The police have officers guarding both crime scenes. We're going to get to the bottom of this. I promise you that," she assured them.

"I talked to Sam," she continued. "He's going to meet you at your house and help you salvage anything that can be saved. You may want all of your daylight hours to work on that. I thought the committee should meet early this evening. Joan offered to make supper for us," she said.

"We can meet here," Maggie offered. "Alex and Marc will be staying with me while we sort all of this out," she added in a tone that indicated the issue was not up for discussion. With an immediate plan in hand, the three men set out and Tonya and Maggie returned to the kitchen to fix themselves breakfast and review the events of the previous night.

Sam was waiting in his truck when John, Alex and Marc pulled up shortly before nine. The driveway was blocked with two police cars and the Fire Marshall's SUV. "They won't let anyone on the property until they finish their investigation," Sam told them as they gathered on the street. "The insurance investigator is there, too. He's the one who told me. Said that they should wrap it up by noon. The security fence will be installed this afternoon and the insurance company will have the restoration folks here tomorrow to help you retrieve anything salvageable. They'll clean it up and store it for you.

Alex nodded. "That makes sense. I want to see if they have any more information on how this happened. Then I guess we need to buy some clothes for the next few days," he said, turning to Marc. "I really need to spend time this afternoon getting my office back up and running."

"I can take care of the home stuff. You work on your office. Let's see if they have anything to report," Marc said, pointing to the group stationed by their front door.

John and Sam hung back as the two men approached the Fire Marshall. "This is bad," Sam said. "I don't know if they were targeted because they're gay, because of our pension fund investigation, or because Alex has made noises about running for mayor against Wheeler. Or all of the above," he concluded.

"I knew we had an old-boy network in Westbury," John said. "I thought they were an incestuous group of glad-handers. I never thought they were criminals."

Sam described the drug deal he observed at the clothing exchange. "They may have their hands in that, too," he said. "They must have known about it. Tim and I got the list of the centers and the names of the owners on the deeds. All of them were foreign partnerships or limited liability companies. Alex was going to find out who owns them."

"It may be time to turn this over to the police," John said. "We can discuss it tonight. Make some decisions." John pointed over Sam's shoulder. "Here they come. Why don't I take Alex to his car and stay with him today. You and Marc can pick up his car and you can help him. They're both exhausted. I don't think either of them should be off on their own today." Sam nodded his agreement.

Alex and Marc reported that the fire started in the kitchen. Everything there was a total loss. The master bedroom was at the opposite end of the house and hadn't been touched by flames but was badly damaged by smoke and water. The restoration company would begin work on Monday. They were given a prepaid credit card to buy necessities immediately. Alex was clutching a plastic under-the-bed box that appeared to be filled with papers. "These are old family photos and letters from my parents and grandparents. All I have left of them," he choked. "By some miracle, they weren't damaged. The police let me take them."

Alex and John headed off to Alex's office, while Marc and Sam turned toward the mall to pick up clothing and toiletries. They promised to meet at Maggie's at five.

Maggie and Tonya decided they should finish the report on the pension fund properties as soon as possible. They both feared that the investigation had made Alex the target of the previous night's violence. The sooner they got the information into the hands of the police, the better.

Tonya called Beth as she was headed to a nearby park to walk her dog. She willingly abandoned her plans and turned back toward home. Tonya and Maggie joined her there, laptops in tow. Maggie spent the afternoon on the internet, researching the owners of the shopping centers. The ones that had been acquired after a recent foreclosure were owned by a series of offshore partnerships or limited liability companies. "We've reached a dead-end on these," she observed. "But we've definitely got red flags indicating fraud. Law enforcement will have to subpoena records to get to the people behind these off-shore entities."

Beth and Tonya spent the afternoon feverishly organizing and inputting data into a spreadsheet. Their efforts documented a sophisticated scheme.

"Absolutely astounding," Maggie cried. "There's nearly twenty-five million dollars misappropriated here," she said. "That's enough to make them do some pretty desperate things."

The women finished up shortly before four. They emailed their report to the committee and printed copies. Tonya set off for home to spend a few minutes with her children before the committee meeting. Beth said that she would stop by Joan's to help her pack up the dinner to take to Rosemont. Maggie returned home and set the table.

The liquor store was closed and Chuck and Ron Delgado were ensconced in Chuck's office, indulging their Sunday afternoon habit of boozing and watching sports. Chuck cursed when he heard the telltale rap on the door below. He thought about ignoring it, but Frank Haynes was not a man to be ignored. Chuck switched off the TV as he buzzed Frank Haynes in.

"Jesus Christ! What the fuck is wrong with the two of you? You had to torch *both* places?" Haynes exploded as he burst into the room. "What the fuck were you thinking?"

"We wanted to create a distraction for Scanlon. He's the only one on their little committee that can do us any damage," Ron replied.

"Two fires? No one will ever believe that these aren't suspicious."

"My guys got their wires crossed. They were only supposed to torch one," Chuck interjected. "We got a two-for-one deal out of it."

Haynes spun on him. "You think this is funny? Instead of creating a distraction, you've upped the ante on the investigation. We're now going to have the cops and the Fire Marshall all over this. Maybe the Feds."

"I've been thinking about that," Ron said. "This may not be such a bad thing. If they're investigating the fires, they won't be looking at the Town's books. Maybe Chuck's created a distraction for both Scanlon and the authorities."

"Yeah, and they may think that Scanlon was a target because he's a queer. One of those hate crimes," Chuck continued. "The newspapers eat that shit up."

"How good are your 'guys'?" Haynes asked. "Will the cops be able to trace anything back to you?"

"No worries, Frank. They're the best. They've been torching stuff in the tri-state area for years. Never been caught."

Good God, Haynes thought. How in the hell did I ever let myself get mixed up with a low-life piece of shit thug like Delgado?

"Don't look so high-and-mighty, Frank," Chuck said. "You're in this up to your eyeballs, just like we are."

"We shouldn't fight among ourselves. We need to keep our heads down and get money back into the pension fund as soon as possible," Ron advised. "We don't need to do anything else that could bring attention to us," he said, looking pointedly at his brother.

"I'm not stupid. I know that," Chuck replied. He turned to Haynes. "We're getting the money together, Frank. You'll see. Quit worrying about it and let us work."

Haynes took no comfort from their assurances, but couldn't think of anything else to do or say at the moment.

The mood around Maggie's kitchen table was somber as the exhausted group sat down to a simple meal of homemade lasagna, Caesar salad, freshly-baked bread sticks, and Joan's renowned lemonade pie. "In a crisis, you need to carb-load," Joan advised.

Sam asked if the group would mind if he said grace. "I've spent the day thinking how fortunate we are that no one was hurt and how much guidance we need on the way forward." Sam addressed his maker with a sincerity and directness that indicated he did this on a regular basis. He ended his prayer by thanking God for this challenge and for the group working together by His grace to address it.

Uplifted by the strength of this gentle prayer and by the pleasure of the delicious meal, tension eased out of the group gathered around Maggie's table. Easy conversation flowed about the first spring flowers and the excitement over the success of the high school basketball team. As plates were cleared and coffee refilled, talk turned to the days' events.

Alex stated that his firm would be able to function fairly normally the next day. His landlord would move him to an executive suite in a nearby building until his office was restored.

The automatic sprinkler had functioned well and the repairs were expected to take six weeks.

Marc had purchased what they needed to get by and was meeting with the restoration company at the house in the morning. The security fence was in place around the house.

Tonya took the floor last, handing out copies of the report and going over it in detail. John was the first to speak. "When you put all of the pieces together, it paints a grim picture of corruption," he stated. "Add in last night's arsons, and I believe we need to turn it over to the authorities. This is more than we can handle on our own," he concluded.

Alex jumped in. "The sooner the better. We can't let anything happen to anyone else."

"Are we all in agreement?" Tonya asked, scanning the room. All heads nodded. "I'm going to call Chief Thomas right now. I talked to him this morning and told him to expect a call tonight. I'd like him to come over and meet with us now. I know it's getting late, so if any of you want to leave, feel free," she offered, but it was clear that no one was going anywhere until the matter had been put safely into the hands of the Chief of Police.

Chapter 17

Monday morning started with a burst of activity at Rosemont. Marc and Alex were up early, anxious to launch into their days. Maggie heard them stirring downstairs, trying not to disturb her. It had been close to midnight when everyone had cleared out and Maggie was able to head upstairs. She decided to get up to see them off and come back to bed for a few hours. She didn't have anything scheduled before her conference call at ten.

Maggie was nestling into her pillow and thinking what a delicious treat it was to sleep in on a weekday when her cell phone rang. She groaned inwardly and was tempted to ignore it. Instead, she picked it up and saw that Susan was calling. It was five a.m. in California and Susan was not an early riser. She swung her feet over the side of her bed and punched the answer button.

"Mom, it's me," Susan sobbed.

"Honey. What's wrong," Maggie asked, fear tracing her spine with its razor's edge.

Susan gulped a ragged breath and continued, "Rob broke up with me last night. Said he isn't sure he can give me what I need, isn't ready yet. Some bullshit like that."

"Oh sweetie," was the only thing Maggie could think to say.

"I knew something was up. He's been pulling away from me for the past several weeks. I asked him if anything was wrong but he just kept saying 'no,' he was busy at work and he was tired. And he's been talking about his ex-wife and how much he loved her. I just wanted to scream at him, 'Yep, she's so perfect that she cheated on you and manipulates the kids against you and made your life a living hell during the divorce that she filed for.' I listened to all of his complaints while he was going through it. And he was the one who pursued me after his divorce. I told him it was too soon. He was the one who started talking about marriage, not me." It was clear that she was picking up steam so Maggie remained silent.

"You'd be proud of me this time, mom. I didn't cry – well, I did a little bit – but I didn't argue or try to talk him out of it. All the time he was talking I kept thinking, 'You idiot. You're giving me up? I'm the best thing that ever happened to you.' If he's too stupid to realize what he's got, he doesn't deserve me." Maggie could picture the resolute line of her shoulders, the confident lift of her chin.

"That's exactly right," Maggie agreed. "I'm so relieved to hear you talking this way. You don't need to throw yourself at anybody. Rob should be too mature for this kind of adolescent indecision. He's weak. You deserve better than this."

"I know," Susan huffed. "And he wanted to 'remain friends'. Like continue to talk and go hiking and stuff. I told him I didn't want there to be hard feelings between us but that I couldn't see us going on as friends. I think that would be too hard on me," she added.

"Why would you want to, for heaven's sake? He certainly hasn't acted like a friend. Pressuring you to commit to him and then deciding he isn't ready. What's that all about? I don't respect that. Between work and your existing friends, you're booked," Maggie said. "Save your extra time for Mr. Right. He's probably waiting just around the corner. Waiting for Rob to get out of the way."

Susan laughed. "That makes me feel better," she said. "You always do. I hate having to start over," she moaned. "And we had big plans for Easter. We were going to stay at a little inn on the beach. I guess I'll go over to Mike's and be with the girls."

"No," Maggie replied. "Why don't you come here. I'm throwing a big Easter bash and fundraiser, and I could use the help. It's going to be right here at Rosemont. And you could get acquainted with Westbury. You must have unused vacation; you never take any. Why don't you stay for a week – or two?" Maggie asked.

Susan was silent for a moment. She's seriously considering it, Maggie realized with surprise. "You know, I think I will come," she said. "I miss you and I want to see where you're living now. The change of scene will do me good. And if I'm out of town I can't see Rob. I know it'll be hard, but I intend to make a clean break of it," she said. "What is this fundraiser for? What are you doing to raise money?"

Those are great questions, Maggie thought. In truth, she came up with the whole idea on the spur of the moment to entice Susan to visit. She knew the fundraiser's purpose would be to raise money for the pension fund. She couldn't raise enough money to have a significant impact, but she could raise awareness of the issues. It would give her a chance to meet more people. And it might convince Susan to visit.

Reconciled to the fact that she wouldn't have time to get any more sleep, Maggie launched into a detailed description of the suspected corruption in the town government and the committee's investigation, the arson fires, and Alex and Marc's temporary residence with her. She left out the part about her dinner with John. She wasn't ready to get into all of that yet.

She admitted that the planning for the fundraiser was still in its infancy. "I saw some great decorations in the window of a charming gift shop on the Town Square," Maggie said. "I decided then and there that I would host an Easter dinner and would buy new decorations for my table. The idea of a larger 'event' just hit me."

"Rosemont's lawn is the perfect location for an Easter egg hunt," she said. "We could have other games, with prizes. Maybe a bake sale with donated goods. The fire department could send over a truck and kids could climb on it and get their pictures taken. Three-legged races. Old-fashioned stuff," Maggie concluded.

"If anybody can pull this off, it's you, Mom," Susan said. "It does sound fun. Very nostalgic, which is how I picture your new home. Minus the corruption and criminal arson," she added.

"Can you think of anything else we could do?" Maggie asked.

"Let me go online and do some research. I'll come up with something. Will anyone else help you on this?" Susan asked.

"I'll have a committee," Maggie answered, and hoped she was right. "Sweetie, I have to get ready for a conference call. Can we talk later?" Maggie asked.

"I've got to get dressed for work, too. I'll make my plane reservations and give you a call. Easter is a week from Sunday. I'll try to come in on the Wednesday before and stay until the Saturday after. Would that be OK with you?" she asked.

"Perfect," Maggie assured her. "Chin up, dear one. I'm proud of you. You're putting your feet onto a happier path. Love you – talk soon."

Chapter 18

When she arrived early Monday morning, Tonya Holmes was surprised to see the cars of the Mayor and other Council Members in the lot behind Town Hall, with the conspicuous absence of Frank Haynes' shiny Mercedes. The mayoral position was full time, but the Council slots were not and most of the Council Members held down other jobs. It was rare for the Council Members to be at Town Hall unless a meeting was scheduled.

As she walked down the corridor she noted that their offices were vacant. She stashed her purse in her desk drawer and decided to find them. She wanted to talk about the fires.

Staff workers were beginning to filter in; hanging up their jackets, putting their lunches in the refrigerator, logging onto their computers. She murmured "Good Morning" to everyone she passed as she continued her search. The large double doors to the suite that housed the Mayor and his assistant were closed but the light was on. If he and the other Council Members were in the building, they must be in his office, behind closed doors. She knocked firmly as she tried the outer door.

No one answered. The door was unlocked and she entered the waiting area outside the Mayor's office. His assistant wasn't at her desk. Tonya heard raised voices coming from the Mayor's office. She approached the door and hesitated, hoping to hear what they were arguing about.

"He told us to take care of things. And we did," she heard, but couldn't identify the speaker.

"That's bullshit," she heard Wheeler spit back. "He didn't mean this. You guys don't know when to stop. I'm out."

"It's not that easy," and this time she knew it was Delgado talking. "You're out if we say you're out."

Others joined the argument and Tonya stepped closer to the door. Wheeler charged out, tossing "Fuck you" over his shoulder as he collided with Tonya. "What the…" he cried. "What the hell are you doing?" he demanded.

"Good morning, Mayor," Tonya answered as she steadied herself. "Gentlemen," she said, as she stepped into the office. "I was surprised to see that you were all here today. And so early. I went looking for you. And here you are," she finished.

They sat there, each one waiting for someone else to break the silence. They're thinking of how to spin this, Tonya thought to herself. She smiled pleasantly and waited for a response.

"We were talking about the fires," Wheeler finally supplied. "Did you hear about them?" Tonya nodded.

"Shocking that such a thing could happen in Westbury," he continued as he warmed to his subject. "We're going to make sure that the Fire Marshall and Chief of Police give this their full attention. These perpetrators need to be brought to justice. Immediately," he concluded. Heads bobbed in agreement around the office.

"I thought that would be obvious," Tonya replied. "Good to know you're 'on it'. It'll be interesting to find out where this all leads. Anyone have any theories?" she asked innocently.

"No," Isaac answered. "No idea."

Tonya nodded as she turned and left the group to wonder what she might have overheard.

At three o'clock that afternoon, Maggie sent out an email to the committee announcing the Easter carnival to be held on the front lawn of Rosemont on the Saturday before Easter, for the benefit of the pension fund. She outlined her basic idea and asked for suggestions and help if anyone had the time. Maggie logged off and decided to go to the Square to buy the Easter decorations she saw in the shop on Saturday.

The bell on the door of Celebrations heralded her arrival into another world. Maggie stopped just inside the entry to inhale the

116

air, deeply scented with the aroma of gardenia emanating from a circular table to her right loaded with candles and oil lamps. Soft, new-age music played discretely in the background. The shop contained a large center section featuring seasonal decorations and housewares, surrounded by greeting cards and invitations. Maggie unzipped her jacket, settled her purse on her arm, and got down to business. This would be the most restorative hour she had spent in a very long time, she was sure of it.

She headed first to a table of ceramic rabbits, right out of Beatrix Potter. They were sitting on a field of shimmery green netting, interspersed with faux colored eggs and nosegays of violets and lily-of-the-valley. She stood back to admire the charming scene. There was something soothing yet invigorating about being surrounded by beautiful displays. The symmetry, color, and textural delight of the produce department at Whole Foods or the towel displays at a department store were like being in a real-world art museum.

The shop was empty and Maggie leisurely examined everything in it, making a mental note of the merchandise they carried for future reference. She circled back to the rabbits and examined each one, arranging them in groupings until she was satisfied with her selections. Other must-haves were plastic bunnies that looked like they were made of chocolate and a handful of pastel baskets adorned with silk flowers.

The shop owner was clearly excited at the prospect of this very large sale. She asked Maggie if she was having a party and Maggie told her that she had just moved to town and would be hosting an Easter carnival at Rosemont to raise money for the pension fund.

"What a super idea," the woman said, eyeing her curiously. "You can put a notice in my window, if you'd like. I'm sure the other shop owners along here would do the same. In fact, Ellen at the print shop would make them for you. And I can donate items for prizes. I'll bet Charlotte next door will give you candy. It's really nice of you to do this. I'm Judy Young, by the way," she said, extending her hand.

"Maggie Martin," she replied as they shook hands. "That would be terrific. I just thought this up and haven't gotten very far organizing things. I didn't think about how I was going to publicize it yet," she admitted. "I still don't know exactly what we'll be doing."

"I can help if you like," Judy offered. "I'd be happy to organize the merchants around the Square. We have a little association, and I'm president. We all love Westbury. We were so glad that you decided to keep Rosemont as a private residence," she added.

"I can certainly use the help," Maggie said. "I'm going to get this all planned in the next few days. Would you talk to Ellen about printing the notices? It will be on the Rosemont lawn, from ten until two. Easter Egg Hunt, games, food, and fun for children of all ages. Donations encouraged for the pension fund."

"How about a silent auction?" Judy asked. "I can organize that. You wouldn't have to do a thing," she offered.

"Fabulous! Can you take care of getting the notices out, too?"

"Of course. We'll post them in the Library and the Town Hall, too, and the vet will put one up in his clinic. He's so nice. Have you met him yet? Good," Judy said as Maggie nodded. "I'll give a stack to my realtor-friend, Tim Knudsen, too. He's all over the place. He'll help. Maybe we can get him to take charge of collecting donations. You can't say no to him," she said. "Why don't you call me tomorrow afternoon and we can compare notes," Judy suggested as she helped Maggie carry her purchases to her car.

This is really going to happen, Maggie realized as she closed her trunk. She decided to walk across the Square to Laura's to pick up muffins to have on hand for breakfast, now that she had guests in the house.

Laura greeted Maggie with an excited wave. "We were just talking about you. Joan and me. You just missed her. We were talking about the Easter carnival. What a great idea," she enthused. "Joan is going to talk to Beth. The three of us will handle the bake sale. I'll donate coffee cakes. And Pete and I will both provide gift certificates to sell at the silent auction."

"Word travels fast around here," Maggie laughed. "I just thought this up and my email only went out a little while ago."

"I know," said Laura. "Judy called me as soon as you left her shop. She'll have talked to everyone on the Square by the time the hour is out. Joan came in as I was hanging up with Judy and she had already read your email. She definitely wants to help. Sam will ask John to work on games and contests. And John has a client that rents out a pony for birthday parties. They might donate it, if you don't mind having a pony in your yard."

"And I thought I had a big job ahead of me. All I have to do is stand back and let it happen. It all sounds wonderful. And a pony would be great," she said. "Judy thought that Tim Knudsen would be willing to take charge of collecting donations. I'm sure I could get Alex and Marc to hide Easter eggs. And my daughter from California will be here, so she can help."

"How nice for you," Laura said. "I can't wait to meet her. And I'm sure you're anxious to show Rosemont to her." Maggie was so engrossed in this happy conversation that she almost forgot the muffins she stopped in for. Her cell phone rang as she was making her selections from the case, and it was Tonya calling to tell her that she would take care of refreshments. Her church had an old-fashioned popcorn popper and large containers for water and lemonade. She would borrow them. "Maggie," she said, "This is just what we need around here to get us out of the doldrums and put some spring back into our step. You're like a breath of fresh air around here. I can't imagine what we would have done without you – on so many levels. Thank you," she said as she punched off the line.

Maggie had just hauled her purchases into the house and was wondering what she would fix herself for supper when her phone rang. "Maggie, its John Allen," said the now-familiar voice. "I got your email about the Easter carnival and I think it's an inspired idea. You have more energy and imagination than anyone I know." Maggie flushed with pleasure. "I've got some ideas and suggestions, but mainly want you to know I'll be available to help with whatever you need. I know this is short notice, but if you haven't eaten yet, I was wondering if you'd like to have dinner with me?"

"Your timing is impeccable – I was just heading into the kitchen. Alex and Marc are working at Alex's office tonight," she told John. "So I'm free." John replied that he would pick her up in half an hour.

Maggie fed Eve, changed her clothes, and printed off the email from Susan with her flight information. John arrived right on time.

"How about Italian?" he asked. "I know a small, family-owned place. The thin crust pizza is remarkable."

"Sounds like a plan," Maggie replied. "I used to eat pizza with my granddaughters all the time. Haven't had it since I left California. When they visit I'll need to know where to go."

Tomascino's was tucked away on a side street running off the Square. The Monday night crowd was thinning out when they walked through the front door that opened directly into the dining room. The young hostess ushered them to a corner booth and a waiter swooped in to take their drink order. As she leaned back into her seat, Maggie stretched her shoulders and stifled a yawn. She thought John looked exhausted, too. Over a California Veggie Supreme, she brought him up to date on the plans for the Easter carnival.

"That's remarkable," he said. "These things usually take months to plan. Shows what you can do when you want to," he observed. "Sam and I talked briefly. We're going to be your games chairmen. Sack races, hula-hoops, maybe something with Angry Birds – whatever those are – Sam knows. And my client with the pony is willing to loan her out if you don't mind having her. She shouldn't do any damage to your yard."

Maggie smiled at him. "I don't mind in the least. I plan to enjoy this property. If it suffers some wear and tear, so be it. Anything in the yard will grow back. I take it you won't mind putting up a sign in your clinic?" she asked. "How many people do you suppose might attend? Any idea how much money we might make? I want to set a goal for us. I'm a big believer in visualizing what you want to achieve. And I want it to be a stretch goal," she concluded.

John considered for a moment. "Well, I suspect at least a couple hundred will attend. People are really curious about your house. You'll get some who will come just to peek in the windows. You could have as many as five hundred," he said.

"I'm hoping that we can raise at least ten thousand dollars," she admitted. "Do you think that's crazy?"

John paused and regarded her steadily, "No. No, I don't. I'll bet that you usually accomplish what you set out to."

Maggie blushed at the compliment. "We'd better get back," she said. "I know you start your day early, and I want to be home when Marc and Alex return. And I need to get ready for my daughter's visit. Susan has broken up with her boyfriend – I'm very glad of that – and is coming the Wednesday before Easter to spend ten days with me. She'll be here to help with the carnival and will go home the following Saturday. I'm so excited she's coming."

"That's wonderful news. I can't wait to meet her. I'd like to take the two of you to dinner when she's here. After the carnival. Would you have time?" he asked.

Maggie hesitated. "I'm sure we will," she said, wondering what she would tell Susan about their relationship. What was their relationship, anyway? "Thank you. And I'm planning to have a small group over for Easter brunch. If you don't have other plans, I'd love to have you join us."

"The day after the carnival?" he asked. "Are you crazy? If you do that, it should be a potluck. I'll come, and I'm bringing a ham. Is that OK?"

Maggie smiled. "That's thoughtful but not necessary. This won't be a fancy brunch. More like a late breakfast with desserts. I've got it covered."

They pulled up in front of Rosemont and he walked her to her front door. "Thank you for dinner tonight and for helping with the carnival. And thank you, again, for the other night. What an adventure. I loved it. I had so much fun skating and the meal was fabulous. But best of all was getting to know you better," she said.

They were alone and the serene night enfolded them. This was the time. John took her in his arms and slowly, increasingly, insistently kissed her. Hesitant at first, she leaned into his embrace and explored the wonder of sensations that only a kiss can produce. When their lips parted, she rocked back on unsteady legs, surprised and delighted that first kisses still held a special magic, even at the advanced age of fifty-five. She stayed put, hoping he would kiss her again. Instead, he gently remarked that he had better let her get some sleep. Disappointed, she bid him goodnight.

Chapter 19

Tuesday flew by in a frenzy of activity. Maggie was busy at work. She also received dozens of emails about the carnival. Judy was as good as her word and organized contributions from the Square merchants. Eileen produced an engaging flyer and by the end of the day it had been posted in dozens of shops and businesses.

Maggie looked up from her computer at two o'clock and realized she was famished. She retrieved a carton of yogurt from the refrigerator and stood at the breakfast room window while she ate, surveying the sloping back lawn and visualizing the carnival in full swing. "We're going to pull this off," she told Eve. "And Susan is coming." Susan was really coming. Maggie lobbed the empty carton into the trash and turned to Eve. "Come on," she said. "Let's go upstairs and pick out a bedroom for Susan."

Maggie had two of the rooms in mind. She wandered through both of them, and settled on the one overlooking the back lawn and library garden. It had a small balcony off of the attached sitting room and the bathroom was charming, with a bay window next to a claw-foot tub. The bed linens and towels had seen better days, however, and it could use some colorful pillows and accessories.

Maggie loved anything connected with fixing up a house and devoted herself to making the bedroom beautiful and inviting for Susan. She spent every free moment during the next week running back and forth to the mall, antique dealers, thrift shops and consignment stores. Her primary color scheme was a restful aqua and cream – elegant and sophisticated. They looked beautiful against the heavy, dark mahogany bedroom furniture and the taupe walls.

She found the perfect Aubusson rug in a floral pattern at a local rug dealer. It was gently used and pricey, but much cheaper than a new rug and would be a stunning focal point in the room. Maggie splurged and bought it. Determined to now stay within her budget, she found an eight-piece duvet set (complete with bed skirt, pillow shams and decorative pillows) at a consignment store and got candlesticks and other decorative accessories at the hospital thrift shop. She secured a donation from each store manager and posted a notice of the carnival everywhere she went. Maggie also found lots of beautiful and useful objects for the rest of Rosemont. With uncharacteristic abandon, she bought everything that struck her fancy.

Like a bird collecting twigs for its nest, she returned every afternoon with a car full of purchases and spent her evening settling each newly-acquired treasure into just the right spot. Rosemont now bore her personal stamp – was more comfortable, more hers. For the first time in her adult life, she had everything the way she wanted it, without sacrificing to keep peace with the opinionated and uncompromising man she had married. It was about time.

Susan looked tired and a bit thinner as she came through the security checkpoint at the airport. Maggie waved and opened her arms. "How are you?" she asked softly as they hugged.

"I'm OK. Glad to be here. I needed to get away from everything and everybody. Actually, I'm pooped."

"I'll bet. You started your day really early to get here. Do you have more luggage?" Susan nodded. "Let's collect it and get you home," Maggie said.

The afternoon was sunny and mild as they made the drive to Westbury. The trees were bursting forth in the vibrant green that only appears in spring. Farmers were working their fields. Daffodils and tulips were in evidence around every home. "Gosh, mom, this is a bucolic paradise," Susan observed. Wait until you see Rosemont, Maggie thought.

Maggie decided to postpone giving Susan a tour of Westbury. Susan was tired and it could wait. She would get her home and give her a chance to nap before dinner. They turned onto the long winding driveway to Rosemont and Maggie felt the anxious excitement of someone bringing their sweetheart home to meet their family for the first time. As they rounded the final bend and the house came fully into view, Susan gasped.

"Oh my God!" Susan exclaimed. "This is incredible, mom. The photos don't do it justice."

Maggie pulled to a stop in front. The proper way to see Rosemont for the first time was through that front door, just as she had done. Only weeks ago, though it seemed a lifetime.

Susan leapt out of the car as soon as it stopped and grabbed her bags. Maggie unlocked the door and Eve bounded out to say hello. "So you're Eve? I've heard a lot about you. You're a friendly girl, aren't you?" Susan dropped to one knee and indulged Eve's effusive greeting. "Ok, ok, I need to get in there and see this place," she said as she gently pushed Eve away.

Maggie held her breath as she closed the door behind them and watched Susan, waiting for her initial reaction. Would it be anything like her own?

Susan stood stock-still, clutching her luggage, surveying the scene before her. She cautiously lowered her suitcase to the floor and stepped slowly into the living room. "Holy cow," she breathed over her shoulder, "I'm in love with this place already. It's gorgeous. Solid. Comforting. I get it now, mom. Why you wanted to stay here."

Gratified and encouraged, Maggie commenced the tour. "Feel free to open doors and cupboards and explore it all later," she said. "I know you're tired. I thought you could lie down and rest before dinner. I was planning to take us to a little place in town. Nothing fancy. Or I can scramble some eggs – breakfast for supper kind of thing. You choose."

"Going out will be fine, mom," Susan said distractedly. "I want to see every inch of this place right now." Maggie smiled. Susan had always been a very curious child. After a thorough inspection of the first floor, they headed upstairs. She saved Susan's room for last.

"I've got Alex and Marc staying here, as you know. I picked this bedroom for you," she said as she opened the door to the room she had so lovingly prepared. "If you would rather have one of the

124

other bedrooms, just say so. My feelings won't be hurt." Which, of course, was a lie. Maggie would be disappointed if she had misjudged her daughter's taste.

Susan whistled softly as she rolled her suitcase into her room. "OMG, mom. This is perfect! I feel like I'm on a movie set. Upstairs/Downstairs. And I'm Upstairs. Look at these gorgeous fresh flowers. Awwww. Thanks, mom."

Maggie gave her a hug and kiss and announced, "This now concludes your official tour of Rosemont." Susan smiled. "Why don't you settle in and come downstairs when you're ready to go to dinner. I have some work to finish up. You don't need to change, we're going casual," she said as she attempted to collect Eve.

"Leave her with me, mom. She's so sweet," Susan said as she scratched Eve's ears. "I'll be down in a bit. I don't feel tired anymore."

Alex and Marc met at Pete's for dinner. For the first time since the fire, both men were relaxed. They were lingering over coffee and dessert when Maggie and Susan arrived.

Pete ushered them to a table by the window. As they were situating their purses and coats on the back of their chairs, Alex and Marc came over. "These are the friends who are staying with me," Maggie explained as she introduced them to Susan. "The ones who suffered those horrible fires."

"I remember, mom," Susan said as they shook hands. "What a horrible thing. I'm so sorry for you."

"We're recovering," Marc said and filled them in on their progress. "And we're excited about the Easter carnival. I'm so glad that you could come out for it. Laura tells me that Alex and I are in charge of hiding the Easter eggs?" Maggie nodded. "Terrific. I thought I would go buy supplies tomorrow."

"I'll get all of that," Maggie said. "You don't have to spend any money on this."

"You're kidding, right?" Alex asked. "We're living with you for free. I think it's the least we can do."

"We were just talking about it," Marc assured her. "We need something fun to focus on. We'll get the candy and get them all set up. We were talking about hiding four or five hundred."

"Seriously?" Maggie gasped. "Do you think we'll get that many kids?"

"If we get one hundred kids, that's only five eggs each," Alex replied. "I think we'll get at least that many. Everyone in my office is going. Our court reporter is bringing her nephew. And the Judge's bailiff will be there with her daughters. This thing has sparked a lot of interest. Maybe we'll do six hundred," he said. "We're going to head home. I'm exhausted." Alex shrugged into his coat and they said goodnight.

"For someone who has only lived here a few weeks, you sure know a lot of people. I always thought dad was the outgoing one. I was worried that you'd be here and have no friends. That you would stay in that huge house all by yourself like you were retreating into a cave. I'd come to visit and find you living with eighty cats and the blinds drawn. The place would look like an episode of 'Hoarders,'" she concluded.

Maggie laughed. "You certainly have a high opinion of your mother's coping skills. This move has been really good for me. I've got lots of friends. Including the vet that takes care of Eve," she continued. This seemed the perfect opportunity to introduce the idea of John to Susan. "We've been to dinner a couple of times. We even went ice-skating. To my surprise, I'm still pretty good."

Susan's head snapped back to Maggie. "Whoa, mom," she said as she held up her palm. She leaned forward and cradled her head in her hands. They sat in silence as Susan assimilated this information. "So you're dating someone?"

"I don't know if we're actually dating. It's no big deal. He's a nice man and a friend," Maggie concluded.

Susan forced a smile. "You're blushing, mom," she observed. "I think you like this guy." She sat back in her chair and let out a slow breath. "You know, I never thought you'd date again. My assistant told me she hoped you'd remarry but I dismissed the idea. She adores you, you know," Susan added as an aside. "She said that you're young and beautiful and so full of life that it would be a shame if you didn't find someone else. I guess I thought that someone might be Eve," Susan concluded sheepishly.

"I'm not marrying anyone, for heaven's sake. I've just gone out with him a couple of times. He's working on the committee, too. He's very nice and good company. In fact, he wants to take us both to dinner next week. Would you like to do that?"

"I most certainly would," Susan declared. "Wait until I tell Mike. He'd kill me if I didn't check out this new man, friend or not."

"Now don't you go exaggerating things or getting Mike all stirred up," Maggie warned in her best "mom" voice. "There's nothing to be concerned about."

They ordered their entrees and spent the rest of the meal chatting about Susan's latest case and the upcoming carnival. Maggie finally broached the subject of her break up with Rob. Susan turned her focus to a car awkwardly attempting to parallel park outside the window. She cleared her throat and faced her mother. "I'm too tired to get into all of that now. I want to talk to you more about it later. I'm OK. I've wanted to call him but stopped myself," Susan said. "I've got questions, but it basically doesn't matter what the answers are. I'm so tired of waiting for him that I'm just done."

Maggie reached over and took her hand. "That's an excellent tack to take. I'm really proud of you. We can talk whenever you're ready." Susan yawned and brushed the hair off her forehead, and Maggie recalled the exhausted little girl that would nestle in her arms and resist sleep to beg for just one more story. Her determined daughter would be just fine. Maggie signaled for the check and was delighted to find that Alex had taken care of it on his way out.

Chapter 20

Alex, Marc and Maggie were all dressed and in the kitchen at Rosemont before dawn on Thursday. The TV morning show nattered away in the background as they quietly and companionably ate their breakfasts. Alex was scanning the paper and Maggie was checking her email. She had postponed all of her conference calls until next week. With only two days remaining until the carnival, she needed to focus on that. The volunteers were all following through on their commitments. Maggie only needed to quarterback everything. She decided to let Susan sleep in. Set-up wouldn't start in earnest until the afternoon.

Eve began barking as Joe Appleby and his landscaping crew pulled up. Maggie shrugged into her jacket and went out to greet him.

"Good morning, Ms. Martin." His usual energetic manner and wide smile seemed a bit more so this morning. "We came early. We're going to spend the day helping you get ready."

"It's Maggie, please," she said as she shook his hand. "You heard about the carnival?"

"Of course. Everyone's talking about it. We'll stay after and help clean up, too. No charge," he added. "It'll be our contribution. We all want to do this."

"That's terrific. Very much appreciated. Are you bringing your families?"

"Oh my gosh, yes. Between the three of us we have ten kids under the age of nine. They're all really excited. And we're bringing some of their friends. And cousins. You'll have a crowd here."

"Good. This has come together at the last minute and I've been worried that no one will show up," Maggie confessed.

Joe laughed. "No worries on that score. Just the opposite. Rosemont will be packed. You'll see," he predicted.

Deliveries began to arrive in the early afternoon. Sam made several trips to deposit folding tables for the bake sale and silent auction. When Maggie asked where he got all of the tables, his reply was a vague, "Here and there. They're all marked on the bottom. Don't worry about it. I know where to return them," he assured her.

Tonya's husband pulled up with a popcorn machine in the back of his truck. He introduced himself to Maggie and he and Joe maneuvered it to its spot by the back patio. Susan appeared after lunch, looking rested and ready to work, in one of Maggie's old sweat suits.

"I see you've made yourself at home in my closet, just like old times," Maggie remarked. "How'd you sleep? Did you get something to eat?"

"Best night's sleep in months. And I had a muffin and a glass of milk. Don't worry; I'm a big girl. If I'm hungry I can get myself something." She smiled over her mother's shoulder at the busy scene on the lawn. "What a glorious day this is," she said and turned to look back at Rosemont. "And what a magnificent setting. Mom, this Easter carnival idea is perfect. Everyone is so excited. I'll bet you raise a ton of money. And it's going to be a blast." She regarded her mother intently. "I'm seeing a whole new side of you."

Maggie abruptly turned to the house, shielding her eyes with her hand. Now wasn't the time to get into this with Susan – if there ever would be a time to get into it – but she was stung by the familiar implication that Paul was the "fun one." She always did the heavy lifting to make Paul's "spontaneous fun" happen. The fact that he accepted all the credit and they thought of her as a dull tool was evidence of the plagiarism that marked their marriage. She blinked back sudden, unbidden tears and rooted frantically in her pocket for a tissue.

"Mom. What's wrong? Are you ok?"

Maggie made an exaggerated show of blowing her nose. "Nothing – just got something in my eye. It's breezy out here." I'm reading too much into this, Maggie told herself. She couldn't do anything about it, anyway. Her kids loved her and if they didn't see her accurately before, they would discover a new side of her now. That was the way it always was with children. They developed a whole new appreciation of their parents when they became adults themselves. It would have to be good enough.

Her reverie was interrupted as Tim Knudsen called her name. She turned and saw him striding across the lawn. He greeted her warmly and introduced himself to Susan. It was evident he was in a people business by his warm, polished manner. "I've got two port-a-potties for you," he announced. "I'll bet nobody's said that to you before," he chuckled. "I thought you'd need them, and I've got a friend in the construction business who's letting us borrow them for the weekend. The crew is here to set them up and they'll pick them up first thing Monday morning. Show me where you want them," he said.

By dusk, most of the supplies had been delivered and set up. Maggie and Susan were on the way to pick up dinner when a police cruiser pulled to the front door. "Oh boy," Maggie muttered, "maybe we need a permit, or a neighbor is complaining already." Susan stiffened her spine and they approached as Chief Thomas stepped out of the car and greeted them with a disarming smile. He told Maggie that he wanted to personally thank her for hosting the carnival to benefit the pension fund.

"I don't think we're going to raise all that much money," Maggie said.

"That isn't the point," the Chief said. "It's the fact that a whole lot of people care. This has lifted morale and means more to all of us than we can express," he said. Maggie smiled and shrugged off the compliment. He continued, "We're going to patrol Rosemont heavily between now and when everything is taken down. We don't want anything stolen. So if you notice police cars in the area, don't be alarmed. And several of our off-duty officers have volunteered to direct traffic and be a presence," he concluded.

"Direct traffic? Do you seriously think that will be necessary? Will we have that many people?" Maggie exclaimed.

"Oh, I think so," the Chief said as he stepped back into the cruiser. "The whole town is talking about it. My wife, daughter and grandkids will be here." With that, he pulled away, leaving Maggie and Susan speculating wildly on how many would attend, did they have enough of everything, and most importantly – how much money could they raise?

Chapter 21

Good Friday dawned with a promise of showers that was fulfilled by mid-morning. Light rain fell sporadically all day. The gray skies did not dampen the mood of the volunteers in and out of Rosemont.

Alex and Marc spent the morning in the library filling plastic eggs with candy and prizes. In the afternoon they donned rain gear and canvassed the lawn, charting the number that should go in each quadrant and debating how many should be easy to find and how many difficult. Eve stuck to them like glue.

Judy stopped by before opening her shop to drop off items for the silent auction. The back of her old Suburban was packed. Marc and Alex helped carry everything through the house to pile it by the back door. Maggie showed Judy the tables for the silent auction on the covered patio. "Unless we have a driving rain," Maggie said, "these things should be fine outside." Judy assured her that they could cope with whatever nature had in store for them and that she and Charlotte would arrive first thing in the morning to set it all up. "I'm planning to be here all day tomorrow," she said. "This is where the action is going to be. I can always run to the store if they need me."

Both Tonya and Tim called. Tonya would be over in the late afternoon to drop off popcorn and lemonade mix. Tim offered to be on call to pick up or do anything they needed. Rosemont was in chaos and Eve was getting into everything. Maggie decided that her faithful companion needed to spend the weekend elsewhere. She called Westbury Animal Hospital and arranged to board her. She and Susan would deposit Eve and pick up groceries for the Easter dinner she had planned for Sam and Joan, John, Alex and

Marc, Tim and his wife, and Laura and Pete. She also wanted to get fruit and pastries to serve the workers who would be at Rosemont in the morning doing the final set-up. Maggie made some additional notes on her grocery list, snapped the leash on Eve, and she and Susan headed out into the drizzly day.

First stop was Westbury Animal Hospital. Maggie told Susan she could wait in the car; no need to get out in the rain. "Nonsense, mom," Susan said. "I might get a glimpse of this mystery man of yours."

"He's not my mystery man," Maggie sputtered. As it turned out, John was with a patient. The technician at the counter told Maggie that Dr. Allen would be taking Eve home with him for the weekend. There would be no boarding fee. Was it my imagination, Maggie thought, or was the technician giving me an appraising glance?

The grocery shopping turned into a bigger expedition than originally planned. The supermarket had most of what they wanted, but not everything. Mother and daughter shared a love of cooking and kept up a constant chatter about new recipes and recent trends in foods; which vegetables were in style right now and which were on the wane. They stopped at two specialty stops on the way home and eventually had everything they needed, and a whole lot more.

It was pouring rain when they pulled into the garage at Rosemont in mid-afternoon. Marc unloaded the groceries while Maggie and Susan put them away. "Is anyone outside, setting up?" Maggie asked.

"No," Marc answered. "Sam called and said that he and John will stop by after work to drop off the games. And Beth and Laura are going to bring over the bake sale stuff they've collected. Alex went to the office for a while and is going to stop at Tomascino's on the way home to get pizza for everyone. And I was just about to take a nap," he concluded.

"Good plan," Maggie said. "This is perfect nap weather. If I wasn't feeling so wired, I'd do the same. You go before you lose the opportunity."

Maggie turned to Susan. "Why don't you go rest, too? You look tired."

"Mom," Susan said. "I'm just like you. I couldn't sit still right now. Why don't we set the table for Sunday dinner? Are we using the formal dining room? It's gorgeous. Have you used it yet?" Susan asked.

"Nope. This will be its maiden voyage," Maggie replied. "Wait until you see the china and linens I've inherited with this place. And we've got all those ceramic rabbits I bought to use as a centerpiece. You're so creative; you can make this gorgeous. If the food doesn't turn out, no one will notice," she teased.

With this happy task in their sites, they set to work. They decided that the rabbits would show to best advantage on a large ivory damask cloth and settled on the Portmeiron dinnerware. Dessert would be served on square Wedgewood plates with a wide gilt border. They placed the last piece of silver on the table and were standing in the doorway admiring their handiwork when Alex came through the kitchen with a stack of pizza boxes.

"Laura and Beth just pulled up in front," Alex said. "Where do you want them to put the bake sale stuff?" He set the pizza boxes on the kitchen island and trailed off to the front door. Susan smiled at Maggie. "Looks like our break is over. Time to launch back into high gear for tomorrow." She turned back to her mother. "This has been such a fun day. I'm totally into it," she said, waving her hand to encompass the preparations around her. "And I'm feeling much better," she smiled and headed off after Alex.

The rest of the evening was a blur of activity. There were so many moving pieces to what needed to happen the next day that Maggie lost track. The volunteers, however, were on top of their areas of responsibility and Maggie decided to quit worrying and trust that all would be in order.

Pizza had been a grand idea. The atmosphere was relaxed and festive. The rain had stopped and the clouds in the night sky were thinning. She took a supply of trash bags outside to stash for use the next day. We're going to have a fine day tomorrow, Maggie realized. She walked to the bottom of the lawn and turned to look back at Rosemont. The house was brightly lit and people were clustered in groups; talking, teasing, gesturing. Laughter drifted down to her. The dining room looked spectacular, all dressed up in its party finery. The house looks happy, Maggie thought. And I'm happy. She wrapped her arms around her herself and inhaled

134

deeply of the crisp air, scented with lilac from nearby bushes heavy with bloom. Cloaked in peacefulness and contentment, she headed back uphill to return to the fray.

Before she could even get through the back door, Maggie was bombarded with questions. She kept one eye peeled for John, surreptitiously looking over peoples' shoulders for him, as she discussed details of the following day. She knew he had extended his office hours until seven that night to make up for closing the clinic on Saturday to help with the carnival. Maggie wanted to introduce him to Susan and see how they reacted to each other. Susan had been very adult and supportive of the idea of her dating someone, but meeting the actual man might be a different story. Why in the world can't these people just figure things out for themselves, she thought impatiently and was immediately sorry for the thought. They were all generously supporting her hair-brained idea. Still, she kept on the move as much as possible. And where in the world was Susan, anyway?

By the time she finally found her, Susan was holed up in the library with none other than John Allen. They had their heads together over Susan's laptop. Susan was pounding away and John was dictating to her. Stacks of paper were neatly arranged on the hearth. They didn't notice Maggie until she said, "Well, here you are. I was wondering where you'd disappeared to. Hello, John. I see you've met Susan."

John winked at Maggie as Susan replied, "Yep. We're working on sign-up sheets for the games. And we've got that stash of prizes over there that John brought," she said, gesturing to a large box in the corner. "We've made a list of which prize goes with what game. You should see what he brought. Very cool stuff. There's art supplies, puzzles and games. You must have spent a fortune," she said and tossed a smile at John.

Thank God, Maggie thought. She likes him. They're getting along famously. I couldn't have orchestrated this any better myself. "When did you get here? Did you get some pizza?" she asked John.

"I've been here about half an hour," John replied. "I brought the prizes in here and Susan and I got busy. I'll get something later," he said.

"Don't be silly. There might not be anything left if you wait. I'll go bring you a plate," Maggie said. "You just carry on." And they were hard at work before she left the room.

Frank Haynes tallied up the week's income at his restaurants and was pleased with the recent upward trend in revenue. He was on track to reach pre-recession sales levels by the end of the second quarter. He swiveled in his chair to check the weather outside his window and was glad it had cleared up. He removed his Burberry trench coat from the padded hanger on the back of his office door, laid it carefully over his arm, and headed to his car.

He frowned at the rain-spattered exterior of his usually shiny black Mercedes. He'd get it washed first thing in the morning. The interior was immaculate and the leather seat welcomed him like an embrace. God, it was good to be successful, he thought. He liked the trappings of wealth. The only thing missing was Rosemont. Once he had that, he'd be set.

As was his custom, he drove by Rosemont before heading home. That idiot woman had cooked up that cockamamie carnival. What a do-gooder she was. How much could she possibly raise? Five hundred dollars? On a good day, he thought. Well...let her have her little party. Maybe it'd be a big flop and she'd get her feelings hurt. Or better yet, someone would get hurt and sue her. That would surely send her sorry ass back to California. He chuckled and relaxed into his seat.

As he rounded a bend in the road, he was presented with a view of Rosemont fully lit and with a steady stream of cars coming and going. The lawn was bustling with activity. Shit. He pulled off the road and strained in his seat for a better view. This was unexpected, to be sure. She might make a success of this thing after all. He'd have to figure out how to turn this to his advantage. A mirthless smile spread across his lips and he punched the speed dial button for Forever Friends.

Within moments, he had the cell phone number of that woman from California who had adopted the dog several weeks ago. He waited impatiently as the phone rang and feared that he would go to voice mail when she finally answered with a breathless "Maggie Martin."

"Mrs. Martin. Frank Haynes here. How are you this fine evening?"

"Fine, thank you. A bit busy – we're setting up for the Easter carnival here at Rosemont tomorrow. Could I return your call on Monday?"

"That's why I'm calling, Mrs. Martin. I've been trying to find the time to call you all week," he lied. "I want to donate door prizes and a larger item." He was winging it here. He always had gift certificates for free items at his restaurants – they almost never actually got used by the recipients – so passing them out garnered him a lot of goodwill for no cost. He'd have to spend some money on something big. He considered all of the activity on the lawn. If this carnival was a big success, he'd get good publicity, and he'd be able to distance himself from the rest of the Council. Put himself more in the camp of that first-class bitch Tonya Holmes. And he'd be currying favor with this Martin chick. This was getting to be a better idea all the time.

"That would be terrific. We'll gratefully accept anything you want to give. It's such a worthy cause."

Haynes cut her off before she could continue with all of that do-gooder bullshit. "I couldn't agree more." He checked his watch – he still had time to get to the big box electronics store before it closed. He'd give out a bunch of bullshit coupons and one really nice, pricey, show-stopping gift. An iPad, if they had them in stock. "I'll be by in the morning to drop them off – about nine-thirty. You open at ten?

"Yes. And thank you so much. We'll see you tomorrow. We're having a continental breakfast here for the workers, so come early and join us. I appreciate your thoughtfulness, Frank" she replied warmly.

Something about the tone of her voice when she spoke his name touched the sliver of decency in Frank Haynes. He felt like he did when he held a stray in his arms – like he was connected, like he belonged. "Christ; I'm getting soft over a woman? That woman?" he cursed. He spun his car back onto the road and headed off to procure his prizes.

Chapter 22

Maggie was startled awake the next morning by an increasingly loud knocking on her bedroom door. She heard the door open and Susan call, "Mom?" She launched herself out of bed as she yelled, "Come in." Good lord, she thought, it's fully light out. What time was it? She could hear sounds from the lawn and knew that preparations were in full swing outside.

"I can't believe I overslept! Today of all days. Eve usually gets me up at the crack of dawn. I didn't think about setting my alarm. I forgot that she wasn't going to be here this morning."

"Don't rush. We're fine. I decided to let you sleep. You looked exhausted last night. Here's your coffee and some fruit and a muffin. You can have your breakfast and pull yourself together and then come down. It's only seven-thirty. I'll go back downstairs. I know where everything is supposed to go. There are plenty of people to help."

Maggie regarded her calm, competent daughter. She was wearing skinny jeans, a gray hoodie over a white t-shirt, and had her long shiny hair piled on top of her head in a messy bun. The look was effortless and stunning. "Ok," she said. "I'll do just that. Once I get downstairs I don't think I'll be able to get back up here to fix my face. I want to look presentable."

"Mom, seriously, you always look good. Don't worry about that. But then I guess you'll want to look nice for Dr. Allen," she teased.

Maggie decided not to engage on the issue of Dr. John Allen and asked Susan if she wanted to come back upstairs to get ready.

"Nope," she replied. "This is as good as it's going to get today." With that, Susan smiled at her mother and shut the door on her way out.

Maggie whipped around her bedroom like the White Tornado from the old Ajax commercials. A compulsive bed-maker, she threw it together in a nanosecond and got showered, dressed and made-up before her coffee could get cold. When she hit the bottom of the stairs, it was like she was stepping into a circus setting up in a new town. People were moving fast, with an air of decisiveness.

The mood on the lawn was jovial, with the exception of the silent auction area. Charlotte and Judy were in a not-so-friendly debate over whether to set reserve prices for the donated items.

"We're here to raise money, not give stuff away," Judy grumbled. "For Pete's sake, Charlotte, you of all people know how cheap some of these folks can be."

"Yes, but we want to sell this stuff, not haul any of it back with us," Charlotte defended herself.

"What do you think, Maggie?" they both asked as she approached.

Oh boy, she thought. I don't want to take sides and get on the bad side of either one of these ladies. "I'm new here, so I'm not really sure. But I've always seen at least a small reserve set when I've attended silent auctions," she said tactfully.

Tim Knudsen joined them to advise that he had a cash box with him and that he and Dottie Blankford from the Midland Bank would be handling all of the money for the carnival. Dottie had a credit card reader with her so people could charge things. "That should help your silent auction," he said. "And you ladies can sign me up for the minimum bid price on everything. You won't have to take anything home. My wife will probably bid on it all anyway. Just take it easy on those minimum bid prices," he teased. "I don't want to be eating cat food for the rest of the year as a result."

"OK, Charlotte, you see? We can set minimum bids now," Judy announced, turning her attention back to Charlotte. "Thank you, Tim," she said almost as an aside.

Tim knew when to make a quick exit. He nodded to Maggie, said "Ladies," and was off down the lawn. Maggie intended to follow his lead but hesitated a bit too long and got roped into a now testy debate over the minimum bids.

"Let's not overcomplicate things," she said. "Unless something is really pricey, I think you should start everything at ten dollars. No one will quibble about spending that for a good cause, and everything is surely worth at least that," she suggested reasonably.

With agreement on this issue, Maggie extricated herself and made her way over to where Sam and John were setting up the games. "We're good to go," Sam called out to her. The three of them surveyed the hustle and bustle before them.

Sam continued, "The bake sale area is ready. Joan and Laura are there and Beth is helping Tonya get the popcorn machine started. I think we've done it," he said with considerable pride.

"Looks like Alex and Marc are still hiding eggs," Maggie observed.

"Let's go lend them a hand," John suggested. As they headed across the lawn, he said, "I hoped to get a quiet moment alone with you. I wanted to tell you how much I enjoyed meeting Susan and how much fun I had working with her last night. She's a terrific young woman, Maggie. Smart, articulate, funny, kind. Whoever broke her heart and let her go is a fool," he observed.

Maggie smiled at him. She was about to reply when Susan dropped down out of a tree not more than six feet ahead of them. Susan let out a whoop of laughter at their startled expressions. She was dusting herself off and straightening her hoodie as Maggie asked, "What on earth were you doing in that tree?"

"Hiding eggs, of course, mom," she said with an exaggerated eye roll. "What else would I be doing? We can't have them all be easy and out in the open. Some Councilman just dropped off an iPad and a bunch of fast-food coupons to hand out at the door. He seemed nice – said he'd be back shortly. We're using the iPad as the main prize for winning the hunt. I wish I could play," she added wistfully.

"An iPad?" Maggie asked. "I had no idea. Frank Haynes called last night. Sorry – I forgot to tell you. He promised to drop them off this morning. This is terrific! The silent auction items were good, too. I'm going to bid on the spa day at The Mill. And baking lessons that Laura is offering. There's also mani's and pedi's and haircuts. All kinds of things. People have been very generous."

"So," John said. "Where are the rest of the eggs? It's almost nine-thirty. We need to get them hidden and be ready to open by ten. People are lining up already," he said, gesturing in the direction of the banner that declared ENTRANCE.

The sun shimmered in a brilliant blue sky at ten o'clock on that Saturday morning. A light breeze kept the temperature comfortable. The grass that had been slippery and wet at dawn was dry and the lawn was packed. Attendance exceeded expectations. Tim sent word that they had admitted six hundred and fifty-three people and he was projecting a generous take on the admission donations. Most families were dropping a twenty in the barrel; very few people were only contributing a dollar. Frank Haynes casually tossed a fifty-dollar bill at the bucket, missed his mark, and allowed a bystander to retrieve it for him. When the young man exclaimed, "A fifty! We don't want to let this one blow away!" Haynes affected a modest tone and assured the man – and two others next to him who weren't listening – that it was nothing. It was the very least he could do for the deserving workers of this fine Town. One of the men caught Tim's attention and rolled his eyes. Tim responded with a slight shrug and rueful smile. If Haynes wanted recognition, so be it. Counting Haynes' fifty, they would collect more than three thousand dollars at the gate.

The start of the egg hunt was delayed by half an hour to allow everyone lined up at the ENTRANCE to get in and in place. Maggie counted over two hundred children, between the ages of two and twelve, lined up to participate. Tonya's husband was on hand to announce the start of the hunt. George Holmes climbed a tree stump and towered his six-foot-six-inch frame over the crowd.

He raised his right arm and announced in a booming baritone, "Ready, Set, Go!", bringing his arm down with a flourish, and they were off.

The hunt was scheduled to take twenty minutes. Most children, especially the younger ones, were happy when they had collected two or three eggs and retired from the field. Ten minutes into the hunt, there were only a handful of children still actively looking for eggs. By the fifteen-minute mark, that number had dwindled to two determined children; a rangy twelve-year-old boy who clearly had the height advantage and a diminutive eight-year-old girl with a mop of blond curls and large glasses. When the buzzer signaled the end, both of them had thirty-one eggs in their basket.

No one had planned for a tie. Marc proposed that they flip a coin for the grand prize, but the girl wouldn't hear of it. "Nope," she said. "Won't work. We should have sudden death like they do in sports," she declared.

Maggie, Marc and Alex quickly put their heads together. This seemed reasonable. They knew that Susan's egg remained hidden in the tree, so there was at least one left to find. The boy seemed to favor this solution, too, so they turned the children lose again with the proviso that they would flip a coin at the end of five minutes if neither of them found another egg. Otherwise, the first to find an egg would be crowned the champion of the First Annual Rosemont Egg Hunt, as everyone was now referring to it.

The girl spotted the bright orange plastic egg almost immediately. She had to climb the tree to reach it, and was not, as it turned out, a natural tree-climber. The boy sauntered over and plucked the egg out of the tree with his naturally long arms just as she was making headway up the branch. The gathered crowd drew in a collective breath. This seemed like cheating, since she spotted it first. But was it really? He got there first. While the onlookers were contemplating this moral dilemma, the boy settled the question by dropping the egg in her basket, to the cheers of the crowd.

George was climbing back onto the tree stump to announce the winner when Haynes stepped out of the crowd and motioned him down. They engaged in a brief conversation and George resumed his post. "Ladies and Gentlemen, Boys and Girls," he boomed. "I've always wanted to say that. I sound like a circus barker, don't I?" He smiled across the crowd. "We've had both a stupendous feat of egg-finding and a moving feat of sportsmanship here today. The winner of the First Annual Rosemont Egg Hunt, with thirty-two eggs, is Miss Alita Firestone. Alita is in the third grade at Horton Elementary. Alita – congratulations – come get your brand new iPad."

Alita, suddenly shy with all eyes on her, had to be pushed forward by her father who finally gave up and accompanied her to retrieve her prize. Haynes, seeing an opportunity for good publicity, stepped forward to be photographed presenting the iPad in a picture that would appear in the Sunday paper.

"But that's not all," George continued. "Thanks to our own Councilman Frank Haynes, we have a cash award for Superior Sportsmanlike Conduct during an Egg Hunt. That award – the generous sum of one hundred dollars – goes to Mr. Brian Gordon. Please put your hands together for Brian," and the crowd went wild. A surprised Brian came forward to awkwardly shake Haynes' hand and happily receive his cash gift. Haynes clamped an arm around Brian's shoulder and kept it there while he posed for another photo.

The crowd disbursed. Haynes was talking to the reporter as Maggie approached to thank him for his spur-of-the-moment donation of the cash prize. She drew up behind him, waiting patiently for him to finish his statement, and was stunned to hear him say, "Yes. We've all come together to make this happen. The merchants and the new owner of Rosemont were one hundred percent behind the Council's efforts to raise money for the pension fund. We couldn't have done this without their hard work. The Council has always had strong backing from the community."

Maggie's shock blossomed into anger. What a weasel. He's taking credit for all of this, she seethed. Haynes had that cockroach-in-the-kitchen-when-the-light-comes-on look when she touched his arm and he turned to find her at his elbow. "Hello, Frank," she said. She turned to introduce herself to the reporter, continuing, "Maggie Martin. I'm the new owner of Rosemont. I was just coming over to thank the Councilman for his contributions this morning. We were thrilled to get his call last night, offering to donate prizes. We weren't aware that the Council even knew about our carnival. We're glad that he came out today to support us." The reporter looked a bit confused and licked her lips. Haynes recovered himself and turned to the photographer before she could formulate a follow-up question.

"How about a photo of our lovely hostess and me, with Rosemont in the background?" he suggested. "I'm sure Mrs. Martin and I both want everyone to know how pleased we are that the community has been so generous in its support." Maggie knew she had lost this round. The newspaper story needed to be about the success of the carnival and not about petty bickering between her and Haynes. When the photographer finished, she leaned in to Haynes and whispered, "We're not done with this. You should be ashamed of yourself for taking credit for everyone else's hard work. They're going to be furious."

"I think you've misunderstood, Mrs. Martin," he said smoothly. "Why don't you let me buy you a cup of coffee tomorrow so we can sort things out. We can meet at Pete's and you can bring that nice dog of yours with you. I like to keep track of Forever Friends alumni," he said and Maggie's spine prickled unpleasantly. Was he trying to use his kindness about Eve as a quid pro quo for taking credit for the carnival? He held his hand up to block the sun from his eyes so she could only see the thin smile directed at her.

A group of children barreled between them and they hastily stepped apart. Haynes dropped his hand and Maggie detected a flash of anger in his eyes before he purposefully resumed his affable expression. "My daughter's in town from California this week, so I'm completely booked. Maybe another time."

He shrugged dismissively and slithered into the crowd.

The games started up at the conclusion of the egg hunt. Children hopped across the lawn in pillowcases. The longest hula hoop spin was won by a woman of indeterminate age from Fairview Terrace, an assisted-living village across town that deposited a busload of seniors itching for a good time. She told the crowd she used a hula-hoop every day for exercise. She certainly had the technique down pat. She continued long after everyone else's hoop hit the ground and kept hers going for an astonishing twelve minutes. The raw egg toss tested the skill of the softball players in the crowd, and the two-legged race was popular with families. All in all, there was something for everyone.

By the end of the afternoon, every item from the bake sale had been sold and, mostly, consumed on the spot. The silent auction winners were announced. Everything brought more than the minimum bid. The winners were lining up to pay Tim and collect their item. A quick tally showed that the silent auction netted more than six thousand dollars – double what they expected. The incessant bickering between Charlotte and Judy came to an abrupt stop and they were now tripping over each other to bestow compliments.

By two-thirty, most of the crowd had departed and the off-duty officers were doing a fine job of herding the stragglers and directing traffic out of the neighborhood. Joe Appleby was as good as his word and he and his crew set to work gathering trash and helping anyone in their path. Once more, the group on the lawn looked like a circus crew, this time breaking camp. Maggie, Tim and Dottie retired to the library to officially tally the take. The silent auction had brought in six thousand eight hundred ninety-two dollars, the bake sale seven hundred twenty dollars, and the voluntary admission donations came in at four thousand six hundred twenty dollars. The total was a solid twelve thousand two hundred thirty-two dollars.

The three sank back into their chairs and looked at each other in stunned silence. The grin that started with Tim migrated to the other two. "Holy cow," Dottie blurted out. "I wouldn't have predicted this in a million years."

"Susan and I set a goal of ten thousand, which we created out of whole cloth. We had no idea how we were going to get there. And now we've exceeded it. I can't believe it."

Tim looked at Maggie intently. "You got all of this up and running in a little over a week. Mobilized all of us. When I first heard about this, I volunteered my time because I like the people you're trying to help. But I didn't think you would even raise a thousand."

"I have to agree with Tim," Dottie said. "The Bank sent me here as a public relations gesture. I didn't think you would need our services. I'm blown away."

"And it was a whole lot of fun," Tim continued. "We could see the day unfold from where we sat and it looked like everyone was having a blast."

"The paper sent that young reporter out to cover it. I can't wait to see what she writes. Which reminds me, I promised to call her with the final tally." Dottie said, stepping away with cell phone in hand.

Tim turned back to Maggie. "You know what? You should run for political office. Maybe the next Council election. We certainly need new leadership. You've got the vision, the will and the knack of inspiring people to action. We need a fresh perspective around here."

Maggie looked at him like he had two heads. "Are you crazy? I've never been political in my life, much less run for any kind of public office. No one knows me; no one would ever vote for me," she laughed. "But thank you for the compliment."

"Don't sell yourself short," Tim responded. "Think about it. That's all I'm suggesting."

George Holmes announced the grand total from the same stump he had climbed earlier in the day to start the egg hunt. His booming voice reached a crescendo when he said, "Twelve THOUSAND two hundred thirty-two dollars!" The assembled group of volunteers whistled, clapped and cheered. Maggie waved to get their attention. George jumped down and he and Alex handed Maggie up onto the stump.

"Thank you; thank you all," she said, gesturing for silence. Maggie glanced over at Tim and realized, with a jolt, that she was literally making a stump speech. She cleared her throat and raised her voice. "I can't believe it, can you?" The crowd responded again with whistles and cheers. She once more signaled for quiet. "Except I really can believe it, come to think of it. I've watched all of you for the past few weeks. You are the most caring, capable group of people I've ever had the privilege to work with. And I've been involved with a lot of community groups." She paused and scanned the crowd. "This is all due to your efforts. You formed a team to help each other and make it happen. You came up with the ideas. Without any input or follow up from me. No fanfare, no attention-grabbing. Just people pulling together for the good of their neighbors. I did the least amount of anyone." At this, a general denial rippled through the crowd. Maggie ignored it and continued. "I'm so proud to be associated with each and every one of you and so thankful I inherited this remarkable house that brought me to all of you. I know that we've got problems in Westbury, but with this kind of energy and ingenuity, we can fix anything. Westbury surely has a positive future with all of you involved. So here's to all of you. Give yourselves a hand," she concluded as the crowd once more erupted.

"Now that sounded very much like a campaign speech, young lady," Tim observed as he helped her down.

Almost everyone and everything had cleared out before dinnertime. Clouds were stacking up in the western sky and rain was forecast overnight. What wasn't hauled away was stashed under cover on the patio. Maggie and Susan talked about starting to prepare for the next day's brunch, but in the end were too exhausted and collapsed in front of the TV. They finally got enough energy to get off the couch and go to bed shortly before nine, promising to get started early the next morning.

Chapter 23

Maggie groaned when her alarm went off Easter morning. She was flat-out pooped. Why on earth had they planned a party on the day after the carnival? Was she nuts or what? And what possessed them to buy all of that food that required so much preparation? Why hadn't they stuck to an easier menu? As usual, the thought that with proper planning she could accomplish anything, was her undoing. This was the evil side of being well-organized. Her reach sometimes exceeded her grasp and she committed to stuff she shouldn't. Well, she'd just have to adjust the menu on the fly. She pushed the snooze button one more time and drifted back to sleep.

Yikes!! It's eight-thirty, Maggie panicked as she looked at her bedside clock. People would be arriving at eleven, and she was way behind now. She shrugged on her robe, stuck her glasses on her face, and raced down the stairs. When she reached the bottom, she was greeted with the aroma of strong coffee and the murmur of cheerful voices coming from the kitchen.

Susan, Alex and Marc were all busily and calmly on task when Maggie appeared. Marc was slicing fruit, Alex was frying up sausage and bacon for Maggie's famous "Smokehouse Quartet" casserole, and Susan was arranging from-scratch cinnamon rolls in the pan for the final rise.

"Hey, mom. I was going to come get you as soon as I was done with these," Susan said, gesturing to the rolls.

"I about had a heart attack when I looked at the clock just now. I can't believe I overslept two days in a row. Looks like you three have everything well in hand," Maggie observed.

"I think so," Marc said, handing her a cup of coffee. "What else needs to be done?"

"Just the sauce for Smokehouse Quartet and the egg casserole. Do you want to make the sauce, mom? Or teach me how. I've never gotten the hang of it. We can throw the egg dish together in a nanosecond and then I think we're ready."

"I'll show you how; it's easy. I feel guilty for leaving you in the lurch while I slept in. Did you get the paper? Is there a nice story about the carnival?"

The three exchanged a nervous glance. "OK. Let me see it right now," Maggie demanded.

Alex handed her the soggy front page and gestured to the bottom left-hand column where a headline announced, "Council Throws Successful Fundraiser for Pension Fund." The picture of Haynes shaking hands with Brian Gordon was featured, with a caption detailing the amount raised. The article continued on page three with quotes from Haynes and a brief mention that Mrs. Martin allowed the Council to hold the carnival at Rosemont.

"What the hell!" Maggie exploded. "This is my fault. I'm so naïve. I overheard him talking to the reporter and taking all the credit. I should have pulled her aside and set the record straight. I thought she saw through him. Well, this is just perfect!" she fumed. "Everyone is going to be furious."

"I'm not sure anything you said would have made a difference," Alex opined. "Haynes has made a fortune from his fast-food franchises and is well-known around here as a philanthropist. He founded and funds the no-kill animal shelter, as you know. And he gives to every charitable cause. Donates gift certificates. Sponsors youth sports teams. The name 'Haynes Restaurant Group' is on most of the uniforms. 'Haynes Gymnasium' at the high school."

"You've met him," Marc broke in. "He's shrewd and relentlessly self-promoting. Knows how to spread his money around and buy people. That's why he always gets re-elected. So many are beholding to him."

"So you don't think he cares about the causes? He's just buying votes?" Susan asked. "What about the shelter? That seems nice."

"You know, that may be his soft spot. He loves animals. He's known for rescuing strays and he's devoted to his own dogs. He attends the games of the teams he sponsors and turns up at charity events. Like the carnival. But I think he's better with animals than with people," Alex replied.

" Does he have a family?" Maggie asked.

"No. He was in a bitter divorce about ten years ago. One of my partners represented his wife. They didn't have kids – should have been an easy matter to divide up the property, but Haynes concealed assets and was hell-bent on leaving her high and dry. It stretched on for years. He finally wore her down and she settled for way less than she was entitled to. Told my partner that she simply had to be done with him."

"What an odd duck. I guess the important thing is that we raised all this money for the pension fund. But it still infuriates me that he took the credit," Maggie seethed. "Enough whining. Let's get this wrapped up so we can all get dressed and back down here by ten-thirty to put stuff in the oven."

When Sam and Joan arrived shortly before eleven, everything at Rosemont was ready. The smell of baking wafted from the kitchen. The predicted rain had materialized and the day was chilly and gray. Maggie lit a fire in the living room's massive hearth and Rosemont was cozy and enticing. John pulled up next, with an excited Eve in tow. He reported that she had gotten along famously with his dogs.

Maggie and Susan set the food on the sideboard in the dining room. The chandelier and candles were lit, and the china and silver sparkled. It all looked spectacular, like something from the pages of *Gracious Homes* magazine. Susan snatched her cell phone and took a couple of photos. "Before it all gets messed up," she told her mother.

Tim and Nancy Knudsen brought four bottles of really good champagne. They began brunch with a toast to the success of the carnival and to the restoration of health and prosperity to Westbury. Maggie later reflected that her first meal in her new dining room had been everything she could have hoped for and more. Everyone complimented the excellent food, but food alone is never enough to assure a successful party. The congeniality of the company made the day. Goodwill towards all was the underlying current. Susan whispered to her mother that she just loved these people and wanted to take them home with her.

When the meal was over, they took their coffee in the living room by the fire. The conversation turned to the investigation.

"Chief Thomas is a good, honest man," Tim opined. "He'll get to the bottom of this. It may take time."

"I just hope we still have some money left in the Town coffers when he's done," Pete said. "So what happens if they arrest the Mayor or some of the Council? Will they have to step down or can they continue in office until they're tried and convicted?"

"Technically, they can stay in office," Alex answered. "Innocent until proven guilty and all that. If they think they're going to be convicted, they may cut a plea deal and resign their seat."

"Then what happens?" asked Tim. "Does someone assume their duties until the next election, or is there a special election?"

"If the Mayor resigns, they hold a special election. If a Council Member goes, the Council can fill the vacant seat for the remainder of their term. Elections are expensive to hold," Alex responded.

"Will you run for Mayor again if that happens?" Maggie asked Alex. He paused and glanced over at Marc. "We've been discussing it," he said. "Haven't decided yet."

"It's up to Alex, of course, but I think he would be the best Mayor this Town ever had. He has a vision for where we can take Westbury in the twenty-first century," Marc stated.

"If you decide to run," Sam said, "I'll help with your campaign however I can. Make signs and put them up, hand out flyers – whatever. I just can't make any speeches," he added hastily.

"We don't have anything to run for yet, but I appreciate your offer," Alex smiled.

There didn't seem to be anything else to add and the conversation turned to Laura and Pete and the happy topic of the baby on the way. By the end of the afternoon, people reluctantly gathered their coats and umbrellas and headed home, restored and uplifted by the congenial day.

John hung back and offered his services as dishwasher extraordinaire to Maggie. She was about to politely decline when Susan responded with a hearty, "Sure. That would be great. Right this way."

Marc and Alex had already started working. Maggie took charge and declared that Susan, Marc and Alex were relieved of KP duty immediately. They had prepared most of the meal and it simply wasn't fair to also clean up. They happily turned in their dishtowels.

Maggie tuned the satellite radio to the Sinatra station and dried and put away dishes as John washed. They worked in companionable silence for a bit, enjoying the music and the immediate gratification that washing dishes can bring. John broke the silence. "You gave a heck of a stump speech yesterday. Have you ever thought about running for office? Have you ever held political office?"

Maggie smiled and shook her head. "Absolutely not. I've never had the slightest interest. I've known a lot of politicians, though. And I've worked on lots of races at the local level. If Alex runs for office, I'll help with his campaign," she said. "How about you? Have you ever held office? Do you have any aspirations?"

John laughed. "No. Not me. My practice keeps me too busy. I work fifty to sixty hours a week right now as it is. And I used to work eighty hours, until I hired a good bookkeeper. If Alex runs for Mayor or Council, I'll help him. Probably just write a check to his campaign fund. He's a good man."

They finished their task and Maggie fed Eve. "Thank you for taking care of her. It would have been a nightmare having her underfoot the last few days." John took off his glasses and rubbed his eyes. "And I think you should head home to get a good night's sleep before the week starts. I'll walk you out. Come on, Eve, let's go say goodbye."

Maggie slipped her hand through John's arm as they walked down the steps and across the gravel driveway to his car. "So what have you gals got organized for this week?" John asked. "Any big mother-daughter plans?"

"Not exactly. I need to work some of the time. I bought the spa package from The Mill at the silent auction yesterday so I thought we'd do a spa day this week. We've been so busy that we haven't really talked about her breakup with Rob. I've been letting her lead the way on that issue. Maybe it's just as well that she's had all of this to concentrate on. She does seem happy, doesn't she?"

"Absolutely. I wouldn't have known she's suffering from a broken heart if you hadn't told me about it. Maybe she's finding that she isn't really as upset as she thought she would be. Sometimes distance gives us that perspective. We find that we're sad about not having what we wanted, but that the relationship we lost wasn't what we wanted anyway. We were just building it up in our minds to be something it wasn't. The person we loved wasn't who we thought they were. That's what happened to me and my wife. She hadn't been the wife I wanted for many years. I mourned the loss of a relationship I never had."

Maggie looked at John intently. "Exactly," she said. "Very well put. I hope I can remember the way you said it if we get into that conversation. I want us to have a bit more calm, quiet time together so she can open up to me if she wants to. Other than that, we will probably do some retail therapy. And Susan is determined to get me settled into a new gym so I can work out again. She's right, of course. I need to do that. I've just been putting it off."

"I'd still like to take the two of you to dinner. Can you work that into your schedule? Say when and I'll make reservations. I know just the place," John said as he pulled Maggie around to face him. She slid her arms around his shoulders and kissed him – a slow, leisurely, lovely kiss.

"Kissing me like that is not the way to convince me to leave," John teased. Maggie gave him a playful shove towards his car and he was on his way.

Chapter 24

Alex and Marc left the house early the next morning. Susan slept in and Maggie tackled the backlog of work that had piled up over the past week. By the time Susan strolled downstairs at eleven-thirty, Maggie had responded to all of her emails and was ready for a break. They set out for lunch and ended up at The Mill. Maggie wanted to check out the Spa and schedule their treatments.

The restaurant was decked out in its Easter finery, with large urns of iris by the entry and bowls of daffodils, tulips and hyacinths on every table. The effect was charming and cheerful, despite the drab day outside. They were both considering the same two menu choices and elected to split the strawberry fields salad and the garden omelet. Susan remarked, again, how much fun the weekend had been and how nice she thought Maggie's new friends were. They spent the meal recapping both, sharing observations that the other might have missed and retelling stories. When Maggie finally settled the check and they wandered over to the Spa, it was almost two-thirty.

The newly-renovated Spa was tranquil and lovely. The placard by the door boasted a meditation room with ten thousand stars on the ceiling. They offered an extensive choice of facials and wraps. The well-groomed young woman at the reception desk eagerly beckoned them inside.

"Hello, ladies. Are you staying with us?"

"No," Maggie said. "I live in Westbury. I bought a spa package at a silent auction on Saturday."

"Oh, at the carnival at that mansion in town? Wasn't that so much fun? My husband and I took our four-year-old and had a blast. He loved the egg hunt. I hope they do it again next year. I heard that it was all the idea of that new lady. Wasn't that nice of her? And I read in the paper yesterday that they collected over ten thousand dollars for the pension fund."

"That nice lady at the mansion is my mom," Susan said, pointing to Maggie before Maggie could stop her.

"No kidding," the receptionist said, regarding Maggie with a mixture of curiosity and respect. "That was so super nice of you." She turned to her computer screen and asked them if they would like to book services. "We're almost full this week. We've had a lot of out-of-towners here for Easter. But after that we're wide open."

"Oh," Maggie sighed. "Susan returns to California this weekend. We were hoping to get in this week."

"I'll tell you what, I'm going to get you in. Would tomorrow work? Say nine-thirty?"

"That would be terrific," Maggie said. "Are you sure you can do this?"

"We take care of our own around here," the young woman replied. "Like you saw at the carnival."

The next morning found Maggie and Susan wrapped in fluffy robes, being massaged, herbal-linen-wrapped, and pampered by the knowledgeable staff at the Spa. By early afternoon, they were stretched out in the meditation room, Maggie leafing through the March issue of *Town and Country* and Susan peacefully contemplating the ceiling of ten thousand colored lights behind a screen that made them look like twinkling stars. Susan turned her head toward her mother.

"I don't even miss him. Rob. I can't believe it. I've barely thought about him while I've been here. I was just lying here, thinking about him and trying to feel sad, and I honestly don't. He was such a pain in the ass for so long and I didn't see it."

"Sometimes you need a change of scene to get a new perspective."

"I know. I'm so glad I came here. I think I was clinging to him because the whole process of finding someone is exhausting.

Going online, having friends fix me up," Susan groaned. "I'm not looking forward to all of that again."

"I know. Starting over can be daunting," Maggie replied.

"Oh God, mom. I'm sorry. What a tactless thing for me to say to you," Susan replied quickly, turning on her side to face her mother.

"It's OK. I'm fine. I'm happy in this new life I've chosen. And I remember that you had a lot of fun when you were online. It was always kind of exciting to see who was new out there. We spent hours analyzing people. Remember?"

"Well, that's true," Susan admitted. "I just want to find my someone. I want to get married and have a family."

"You will. You'll find each other and all the waiting will be worthwhile."

Susan sighed as Maggie rubbed her back.

Across town, in the grand jury room at the Courthouse, indictments were handed down charging Mayor Wheeler with fraud, embezzlement, and related malfeasance. Although evidence was presented against two other Council Members, the grand jury failed to return indictments against them. Westbury's finest pulled up at Town Hall and led a vociferously protesting Mayor Wheeler off in handcuffs.

By the time Susan and Maggie got dressed and checked their phones, Maggie was shocked to see that she had thirty missed calls and fourteen messages, all from members of the committee. She punched in Tonya's number before she listened to her messages.

Tonya picked up on the first ring. "Maggie – I've been trying to reach you. Have you heard? Wheeler has been indicted and arrested. Hauled out of here in handcuffs about thirty minutes ago. All hell is breaking loose. Are you near a TV?" she asked.

"No. Susan and I have been at the Spa at The Mill all day. We just left and turned on our phones. I had a bunch of missed calls and messages. I returned yours right away. I was hoping to hear this."

"If you're still there, get to the bar and check the TV. I don't think he knew this was coming. Wheeler was belligerent. I was in

156

my office when the cops showed up. News that they were here spread through the building like wildfire. I was in the hall outside his office about thirty seconds after they arrived. He was arguing with them. I actually wondered if he was going to resist arrest. If he hadn't been so angry, I bet they wouldn't have put him in cuffs."

"What a scene it must have been. We're walking over to the bar now. Where any of the other Council members there?"

"Just Russell Isaac. He was quiet and had that deer-in-the-headlights look. Maybe relieved that he wasn't arrested, too. He may be involved. I don't know what to think about him."

"No Frank Haynes?"

"No. He's rarely here unless we've got a meeting scheduled. I know you're mad that he took credit for the carnival, but he is a politician. Comes naturally to most of them, I think. I don't know how I feel about him. All of his kindness to animals makes everyone think he's a nice guy. But I've always found him a bit odd and hard to relate to. He's not well-liked by the staff at Town Hall, I can tell you. I'm assuming that they didn't have enough on any of the others to arrest them. We'll see what develops now that they've got Wheeler. Maybe he'll talk to cut a plea deal. Stay tuned."

"What's next? Who's in charge down there?"

"Not too sure. I've been trying to find out. I called Alex, but he's in court this afternoon. Our Town uses an outside law firm as its attorney. I know the firm has been called. I suspect we'll have an emergency Council meeting tonight. This is all happening pretty fast. Listen – I have to go. Keep your phone on you, OK?" Tonya hung up.

Susan drove as Maggie concentrated on listening to messages and returning calls. They flipped the TV on as soon as they walked through the door, but there was no additional coverage after the arrest and a short news conference where Chief Thomas made a statement announcing the charges. He did not take any questions. There was nothing more they could do or find out.

Susan started dinner and Maggie returned to her office to half-heartedly check her email. After dinner, they spent a restless evening trying to find something interesting on TV. They were watching back-to-back episodes of people buying the contents of abandoned storage lockers and making a mint off of the treasures they uncovered when Marc and Alex came home.

"Can we switch back to network?" Marc asked. "They're about to break in with a statement from Town Hall."

Maggie hurriedly grabbed the remote and tuned in as Chief Thomas and the remaining Council filed in behind a microphone. Tonya was on the far left of the screen and didn't look too happy. Frank Haynes was at the other end. He looked like the cat that ate the canary. A man in a well-cut suit who she didn't recognize stepped up to speak.

"Good evening. I'm Bill Stetson, with the firm of Stetson & Graham. Our firm represents the Town of Westbury. As you know, Mayor Wheeler was arrested this afternoon after the grand jury indicted him on charges that were detailed earlier by Chief Thomas. I'm here to address the effect of this arrest on Town government. Pursuant to the Town Code, the Mayor retains his seat but is placed on paid administrative leave pending conviction or acquittal. Mayor Wheeler may not participate in any way in Town government. In the interim, the remaining Council is empowered to make all decisions and is tasked with selecting one of their members to serve as Acting Mayor. The Council voted this evening and elected Councilman Russell Isaac to serve in this capacity."

Marc exclaimed, "That little twit? But at least he must be honest. Surely they know he's not tied up with any of this."

"Not necessarily." Alex replied. "The grand jury may have considered evidence against him. Just didn't have enough to indict him. Isaac is the most senior person remaining on the Council, so he's the logical choice," Alex said.

The attorney continued, "At this point, I'd like to invite Acting Mayor Isaac to say a few words." An uneasy-looking Isaac stepped up to the microphone. He unfolded a crumpled sheet of lined paper and composed his face into what he must have felt was a humble, thoughtful expression. He glanced at the paper and began in a shaky voice, "Fellow citizens of Westbury, this is a dark day indeed." He turned to acknowledge the other Council Members lined up behind him with a nod of his head and continued, "We will devote ourselves to resolving the crisis facing our Town. We ask for your patience, and your prayers, in the days and weeks ahead. Rest assured, we'll work together to represent the people of Westbury to the best of our ability." Isaac smiled weakly at the press as he edged back to allow Chief Thomas to take his place.

"Mayor Wheeler is represented by counsel and has posted bail. He will be released shortly. This is an ongoing criminal investigation and I can't discuss anything further."

Attorney Stetson announced that this concluded the news conference and they wouldn't take any questions. The Council and the Chief filed out of the room, with Russell Isaac nodding and waving tentatively to the cameras as he left.

"Now what?" Marc asked.

"If Wheeler is convicted, or steps down, they'll have to hold a special election," Alex replied.

"If they're smart," Susan interjected "and if they think it's likely that he'll be convicted, or that too much dirty laundry will get aired during the trial, he'll resign now. Holding the special election sooner rather than later will be to their advantage. Gives the opposition less time to organize a campaign. And less opportunity for damaging information to surface. The longer they delay, the better it is for the other side."

"Exactly," Alex said. "I talked to Tonya about whether she wants to run. She won't risk losing the one truly independent voice we have on the Council right now. So she's going to stay put."

"Makes sense," Maggie said. "What about you? Will you run?"

"Yes. If I can collect enough signatures to get on the ballot, that is. Marc and I discussed this. The timing is lousy. Our house won't be ready for months, but at least my practice is back to normal. We're moving into our old location next week."

"This is a critical time for the Town," Marc said. "We need Alex's vision. I can take care of the house. That's small stuff, compared."

"I couldn't agree more," Maggie said. "And I'll work on your campaign, if you'd like. I've been part of local races before. We can get you on the ballot, I'm sure of it. Why don't we start working on your campaign slogan and platform so we're ready to go if Wheeler resigns?"

"I was hoping you'd offer," Alex replied. "I'll be a long shot. We'll have to work night and day to pull this off," he warned.

"Sounds like my kind of deal. Count me in," Maggie assured him. With a call to action at hand, they all headed off to bed.

Chapter 25

Maggie was busily working at her computer the next morning when Susan appeared, fully tricked out in workout clothes. Oh no, Maggie thought.

"Mom, go get dressed. I went online and found a gym near here. It's off the Town Square. When the weather is nice, you can walk. They have a class in an hour that I think we should try. It's three days a week and it'll be perfect for you. So let's check it out."

Maggie groaned and was beginning to object when Susan cut her off. "Nope, don't even start with me. This is for your own good and you know it. Come on. Chop chop."

Three hours later, an invigorated Maggie and a vindicated Susan were walking back home. "You were right. That class was just what I needed. I'm so out of shape. I'll be sore and cursing you tomorrow. But it felt good."

"You'll keep at it?" Susan asked. "I want you to stay healthy and well for a long time."

"No worries," Maggie assured her. "I'll keep at it. And I'm not that old, you know."

As they turned the corner and came out onto the Square, they spotted two TV news trucks in front of Town Hall.

"What now?" Maggie asked.

"Let's go see. We're right here," Susan suggested.

"Looking like this? I don't have any makeup on. And I was sweating like a pig in there."

"Oh, mom. You always look gorgeous. You don't even need makeup. And nobody's going to be looking at you anyway."

They climbed the steps of Town Hall and entered the large, high-ceilinged foyer. A group was gathered by a podium set up off to one side. They were all waiting for someone. Susan spotted Tonya, who waved them over.

"Wheeler's lawyers set this up," she leaned in and told them. "We're expecting him to resign. There will be a special election. Alex will run. We'll start today to gather signatures to get his name on the ballot."

Before either of them could respond, Wheeler entered the room, flanked by Russell Isaac and two of his lawyers. Wheeler stepped to the microphone and, as anticipated, resigned. He read a prepared statement avowing his innocence, thanking the citizens for their support, promising to fight the false charges brought against him, and endorsing Russell Isaac. The assembled group greeted his remarks with stony silence. He was visibly shaken by the chilly reception and stepped away from the microphone.

Bill Stetson, who had been standing at the far side of the room, now took over. "Ladies and Gentlemen. The Town Code provides that a Special Election must be held within sixty days and that anyone qualified to run for the office must submit a petition signed by three thousand registered voters in order for their name to appear on the ballot. Petition forms are available in the Clerk's Office. The Special Election will be held the third Tuesday in May. More information will be forthcoming. I believe Mr. Isaac would like to say a few words."

"I can't stomach any more of him," Tonya said. "He'll be announcing his candidacy. I'm outta here."

Maggie and Susan stayed put. "I want to assess the opposing candidate," Maggie whispered to Susan.

"Citizens of Westbury," Russell Isaac began, "I'm honored and humbled by the opportunity to serve our Town as Acting Mayor. I believe the charges leveled against Mayor Wheeler are false," he said as he turned toward Wheeler. "I admire the Mayor for stepping aside in the best interests of the Town. We've got a lot of work to do, and I promise you I'm devoted to solving our pressing economic problems. I've decided to run for Mayor in the Special Election. I'll be asking for your signatures on my nominating petitions and your vote in May. Together, we can steer

Westbury to a bright future. Thank you all for coming," he concluded.

Someone has been coaching him on his public speaking, Maggie surmised. He was pompous and oily, but had powerful allies. He would be hard to beat. She picked up the petition form and headed home to get started.

At seven that evening, fifteen people squeezed themselves into the conference room at New Way Realty to organize Alex Scanlon's campaign. "You people sure know how to mobilize," Susan whispered to her mother. "I thought this town was going to be boring."

"Yep. It's a regular Peyton Place," Maggie answered. "Oh, never mind," she replied to Susan's quizzical look. Could she really not know about Peyton Place?

Alex cleared his throat and took the floor. "Thank you all for coming. We've got a lot of work to do to win this election. This is a turning point for Westbury. We can't fail. With your help, we won't." The group turned encouraging eyes on the speaker. "Our first priority is to gather three thousand signatures. Sam and Joan are going to collect them from Town employees. Anyone with money in the pension fund should want a change."

"We think we'll get half of the signatures we need from employees. We're going to hold at least two meetings and others have volunteered to circulate petitions," Sam interjected.

"I'll carry a petition with me wherever I go," Tim said. "We've got the regional realtors' meeting next Friday. I'll have it available at my open houses. I'll be able to get two or three hundred signatures."

"Pete told me he'll circulate them at his restaurant. I'll take petitions to the shopkeepers on the Square and ask them to put them by their registers. And I'll have one at my reception desk," John promised.

"We plan to spend the day at the mall tomorrow. We'll have time to get signatures there," Maggie was surprised to hear Susan say. She caught John's eye and they smiled at each other across the room.

"Terrific. Thank you all. Send me an email at the end of each day so I can keep a running total. We want to shoot for an extra five hundred signatures, in case some of the signers aren't eligible voters. I've heard from a number of lawyers and accountants I know and they're helping, too."

"When will you announce your candidacy?"

"Today is Wednesday. Ideally, I'd like to have the necessary petitions signed by next Monday and confirm with the Clerk that my name will be on the ballot. Then I can get press coverage and would like to make my announcement on live TV Tuesday morning. So that's what we're shooting for."

"We should be able to make that happen," Sam said. "What help will you need after that?"

"This will be a fast campaign season. Which is good because I don't have much of a war chest. Maggie has offered to be my campaign manager. Would you like to address this, Maggie?"

"Sure. Fortunately, the climate in Town right now favors change. We don't want to underestimate Isaac, however. And for all we know, he's knee-deep in this corruption. Some of the voters will see him as experienced and capable. There are also voters who won't vote for a gay man, under any circumstances. Sad, but true," Maggie stated.

"Here's how we get Alex elected. We post campaign literature on every doorknob in town. We'll need lots of help to do this. Ellen offered to print door hangers at cost. We arrange to have Alex speak to groups as often as possible – every night of the week and all day on Saturday and Sunday. Please ask any group you're involved with to invite Alex to speak to them. Consider hosting a "meet the candidate" event in your home. You don't have to provide refreshments. If you do, coffee and cookies are enough. Invite your neighbors and co-workers. I'm going to have Sunday afternoon chats with the candidate at Rosemont until the election. If we have more speaking opportunities than Alex can attend, I'll go in his place and talk up his platform. Would anyone else like to do that?" she asked. Maggie had never seen so many people shake their heads "no" so quickly.

"Oh, come on," Maggie said. "It's fun to do. You'll be surprised at the people you'll meet and how much you'll learn. This campaign will be exhausting and exhilarating at the same time. Tonya plans to get the election board to sponsor a candidate's debate. The media should cover it. Television advertising is too expensive, but we're hoping to get Alex interviewed on local TV and radio stations. A pretty simple strategy, really," Maggie concluded.

"I'll bet that I speak for everyone here. We're with you all the way. Whatever you need, just ask. You're a brave man to take this on," Tim said.

"Ok," Alex declared. "That's the plan. Let's get these petitions signed. Maggie and I will be busy creating our platform. I've already started on my talking points. I promise you that I'll work as hard as I possibly can. I appreciate your confidence and support. I won't let you down."

John collected his petition form and made his way over to Susan and Maggie. "So, ladies, you've got a mall day planned for tomorrow? Sounds exhausting. I'm guessing you'll be way too tired to cook. How about I take you out to dinner?"

"That would be awesome," Susan replied before Maggie could even open her mouth.

"I'll pick you up at seven. And since you're becoming an activist, I think I'd better take you to the hangout long favored by local politicians. Seafood and steaks. And cigars, if you want them. Will that be ok?"

Maggie laughed. "I'm not an activist, and yes, it sounds great. See you then."

Chapter 26

Maggie and Susan left behind a soggy day for the amped-up halogens and oxygenated air of the mall, where it's always bright and cheerful. The stores were full of colorful, easy spring clothes. They spent the morning trying on armloads of dresses at a local boutique. Susan had no luck, but Maggie was having one of those magical shopping days where everything fits, looks great, and goes together. They finally lost track of how many things she had piled up at the register. "For heaven's sake, mom, you're in the 'zone.' Just go with it. You haven't treated yourself to anything new for over a year. Your wardrobe is so business-y. You need some fun stuff. Get it all and take it home to think about it. You can always return stuff. I'm telling you, the shopping gods are smiling on you."

Maggie reluctantly followed her daughter's advice and sheepishly loaded her shopping bags into the back of her SUV. Where in the world did she think she was going to wear all of this? She locked her car and turned to Susan. "We promised, so let's find out where we can collect signatures."

The bored-looking young man at the information desk said that he didn't really know (and obviously didn't care) but thought that they could stand by the east entrance, near the food court. They had shopped through lunch so they bought a snack to tide them over until dinner and solicited signatures from shoppers for the next two hours. Most people were aware that Wheeler had resigned but didn't know that there was going to be a special election. Some were interested in details about the process and who Alex was and what he stood for, while most just wanted to sign the petition to help these pleasant women and get into the mall to do their shopping. Either way, they were pleased to have collected one hundred and eight signatures by the time they headed home to change for dinner.

The rain had stopped and the evening was warm as a caress. Maggie decided to wear one of her new dresses. It was a shimmery coral, with a halter neckline surrounded in coral and turquoise beads. Susan had insisted she buy it. She rummaged around in her closet for her dark coral pashmina to throw over her shoulders and slipped on strappy high-heeled sandals.

Maggie appraised herself in the mirror. She had to admit, she looked good. Like her mother before her, she was aging well. Pretty as a young woman, her mother had really pulled away from the pack in her later years. A good trait to have inherited, she thought. She couldn't shake the feeling that she was overdressed – like she should be on a cruise ship – not going to dinner on a damp Thursday evening after Easter. She decided she would change into something less fancy when the doorbell rang, Eve started barking and Susan yelled, "He's here!"

Drat! It was twenty of seven. Why on earth was he so early? She had expected him to be late, what with finishing up at the clinic and all. Susan burst into her room as she was trying to reach the zipper. "You look fabulous! What are you doing? Don't take that off. It's perfect. Come on. John's here. And I'm starved."

John was handsome in a charcoal suit and silver tie. Maggie let the wrap slip to her elbows and was rewarded with an appreciative glance. Being noticed by a man when you're wearing a new dress never gets old.

"You look lovely, both of you," he said as he gave Maggie a kiss on the cheek and extended his hand to Susan. He flushed as she took it and pulled him in for a hug. Maggie smiled at the two of them. "Did you get any of these beautiful dresses today?"

"Mom did," Susan replied. "She scored big time. I think she can wear something new every day for the next month. That sales lady now has a new best friend."

"It wasn't that bad," Maggie protested. "But luck was in my favor today, I have to admit. And we collected one hundred and eight signatures on our petition," she said as they climbed into John's car. "How was your day? Did you get anyone to sign?"

"Busy day. I knocked off a bit early so I could get myself cleaned up to take two beautiful women out to dinner," he said, turning to wink at Susan. "We collected a dozen signatures. Almost everyone who came in signed. We don't have that much traffic. I talked to Pete. He took petitions to the other businesses on the Square and they all have them at their registers. Have you talked to Alex today?"

"No. He hasn't come home yet. It'll be handy with him living at Rosemont during the campaign. We can have midnight staff meetings every day."

John swung the car into an alley that ran between two old brick buildings and pulled into a parking lot behind a non-descript looking restaurant. A small sign by the back door bore its name – *Stuart's* – and declared, "You're here. Come on in through our kitchen."

John gave the car to the valet on duty and they entered the turbulent kitchen where a trio of cooks worked frantically. Waiters literally ran in and out of the swinging doors at the other end of the room, shouldering trays loaded with plates of steaks, chops and seafood. The aromas of beef and garlic and baking bread engulfed them. They filed along a runner that led past the chaos of the grill to the quiet, dark-paneled dining room. The tuxedoed host led them to a high, upholstered booth along one wall away from the kitchen.

"Good," John said. "This is right where I asked that we be seated. You can see into the bar and the whole restaurant from here. This place is the good-ole-boy bastion in this town. Most of the major business deals have been struck here. Political futures have been born. And if a man wants to escape from his wife, he comes to the bar and if she calls, the bartender says that he hasn't seen her husband in weeks. Not that I endorse that, mind you. Since you're going to be a political mover and shaker in Westbury, you'll need to be known around here," he concluded.

"Honestly, I don't know why everyone keeps referring to me that way," Maggie laughed. "I'm most certainly not a mover and shaker. I'm just a helper."

168

"Come on, mom," Susan said. "I never would have believed it if I hadn't seen you in action this past week, but you are a politico. Look how you created that carnival to raise money, and now you're managing a political campaign. I always knew you were super organized. Mike and I used to complain about it at times, but it's a helpful trait and now I'm just like you that way. What I never saw is how capable you are. I guess you were always in dad's shadow. I'm sorry that we never gave you the credit you deserved."

Maggie shifted in her seat and tugged at the wrap that had slipped off one shoulder. She had longed for this moment – this recognition from her children – for an eternity and now that it was unexpectedly upon her, she was rendered speechless. She flushed with equal parts frustration at herself and pleasure at the remark.

"And another thing," Susan continued. "I thought that you were insane, moving to this hick backwoods. Meaning no disrespect, John," she added hastily. "But I haven't felt this engaged and involved in years. I can see why you care for these people so much. The ones I've met would do absolutely anything for you. I can't wait to hear how all of this turns out. I'm going to call you daily, mom. And if I can do anything at all from my end, you just let me know. I'm so sorry that I have to go back home on Saturday and leave you with all of this."

They were well into their main course when Frank Haynes and Russell Isaac stepped up to the bar. They were starting in on a couple of martinis when Frank noticed Maggie's intent gaze. He nodded at her and whispered something to Isaac. Isaac reluctantly set his drink on the bar and followed Haynes to their table.

"I wanted to come over and say hello to my favorite vet and our new political power broker. And to introduce her to our Acting Mayor, Russell Isaac." Maggie, John and Susan all stood for the round of introductions.

"Sit, please. We don't want to interrupt. Nice to meet the lovely daughter of our mysterious new resident," Haynes crooned. He was curious about Susan. Another tedious career woman, no doubt. He was about to address her when Isaac spoke up.

169

"I understand you're running Alex Scanlon's campaign," Isaac interjected. "Fixing up Rosemont, organizing that little carnival, and now this. Quite a busy lady. Well, this campaign will give us a chance to get to know each other over the next few months. That is, if Alex can get enough signatures to get on the ballot. Just remember, I'm Acting Mayor, so I represent you. My door is always open if you need anything. It must be difficult for you, what with being so new to town. You probably don't even know your way around yet."

"Thank you so much for coming over," Maggie replied sweetly. "I've got a few things I'd like to discuss with you. I'll take you up on your offer and come see you tomorrow. I've got lots of unanswered questions about this Town. And its finances. As for finding my way around? Don't worry; my GPS system takes care of that." She raised her chin and leaned forward imperceptibly, locking him with her gaze. "I'll see you first thing, say nine o'clock?"

Isaac took a step back and stiffened. "I'm not sure what's on my schedule tomorrow. Just call my secretary and she'll set something up," he blustered.

Haynes shot Maggie a look of pure venom. This broad was certainly full of herself. Sensing that Isaac's thin veneer of cordiality was about to crack, he took his candidate by the elbow. "We'd better get back and let you enjoy your dinner," he said as he led Isaac back to the bar.

"Good going, mom. You stood up to that pompous twit."

"He may be pompous, but he's not a twit. I just caught him off guard. He won't underestimate me in the future," Maggie replied. "We've got a fight on our hands."

"I think he's got a fight on his hands," John said. "My money is on you. And I'm here to help you in any way I can."

They finished the meal with lively conversation about books and movies, and the best shows on TV this season. It was late when they pulled up in front of Rosemont. Susan hugged John and thanked him for dinner, then tactfully disappeared through the front door.

"She's great," John said. "And she seems happy and relaxed after this week with you. She'll be fine. Some smart guy is going to come along and realize what he's got in her."

170

"I hope it's soon," Maggie sighed. "She's been waiting so long. I just want her to be happy."

Maggie and John had been drifting together as they talked. They came together in an easy kiss that quickly turned passionate. Maggie pulled away first. "I shouldn't be standing on my front porch necking while my daughter is waiting on the other side of the door. And you've got an early day tomorrow. Thank you for tonight."

John leaned back and smiled down at her but didn't let her go. She continued, "Susan leaves Saturday morning. Would you like to come to dinner here Saturday night?"

"I'd love to, but why don't I take you out? Won't you be tired from all this campaign-running you're doing?"

"No, I'll be fine. I like to cook. It's relaxing and creative. I'm planning to collect signatures at the supermarket on Saturday, so I'll be right there to pick something up for dinner. It won't be fancy, so don't get your hopes up too high."

"Whatever you want to do works for me. And if Saturday comes and you're tired, my offer still stands."

He must be the most thoughtful man on the planet, Maggie reflected, as she stepped across her threshold and locked up.

His mind worked overtime as Frank Haynes drove home after the encounter at Stuart's. Russell Isaac was certainly no mental giant. Being Acting Mayor was going to his head. Isaac understood that he couldn't go it alone; that he needed the support and guidance of Frank Haynes. He smiled in spite of himself. That's exactly how I like my politicians – dumb and dependent – on me. He's expendable. I can frame him, if I have to. Just like Wheeler.

A bigger problem was Maggie Martin. Or more accurately, her ownership of Rosemont. He was surprised to see her with John Allen. The vet was one of the few people in Westbury that Haynes liked and respected. He's certainly wasted no time in courting the wealthy new widow in town, he thought. Not that John would be dating her – if that was even what they were doing – because of her money. The vet was too honorable for that. Well, let him have her. He didn't want another woman in his life, poking around in his personal affairs, trying to sensor his activities, and taking half of his estate when she finally gave up trying to change him. That part of the bargain Dr. Allen could have. But he still needed Rosemont.

Haynes had been absent-mindedly picking up speed and was heading into a curve too fast. He stepped on the brakes and fine German engineering came to his aide, preventing a skid. He straightened the wheel and slowed to the speed limit. He switched radio stations and tried to get interested in the final innings of a Cubs game, but the subject of Maggie Martin wouldn't leave him. She hadn't been in Westbury all that long, he reasoned. She and Rosemont and Westbury were still in the honeymoon stage. There was plenty of time for this new adventure to turn sour. Maybe that daughter of hers would produce a grandchild and she'd want to go back. Or maybe the budding romance with the good vet would fizzle and she'd throw Rosemont on the market and flee back to California with a broken heart. Haynes began to whistle a tuneless melody. All would work out. He simply had to be patient and wait for the parties to paint themselves into their respective corners. If you allowed people enough rope, they inevitably hung themselves.

Chapter 27

Friday passed too quickly. Susan insisted that they work out in the morning. They took in a matinee movie and then explored the shops on the Square. Maggie proudly introduced her daughter as they made their rounds.

Alex returned to Rosemont late Friday evening as Maggie was setting up the coffee pot for the next morning. He stretched his lean frame against the kitchen counter and announced that they had over twenty-five hundred signatures.

"We're going to get there this weekend," Maggie said. "I talked to Sam. He's arranged a meeting of Town workers tomorrow afternoon. He wants you to speak to them. He'll collect signatures there and I'll get more outside of the grocery store after I drop Susan off at the airport. So...congratulations."

"Thanks, I think. When can we have door hangers made up?"

"I've got samples for you to look at. As soon as the Clerk confirms that you're on the ballot, we'll get them printed. We'll have them in hand by the end of next week. We should mobilize volunteers to distribute them. We'll do an email blast as soon as we hear from the Clerk."

"My office has the mailing list done. We'll be ready."

"Has anyone else petitioned to get their name on the ballot? We don't want Isaac to get elected because the opposition vote gets split up."

"Not that I've heard. Most of the people I've talked with think Isaac is a shoe-in. We've got an uphill battle. You know that, don't you?"

"Uphill battles are my specialty," Maggie assured him. "We're going to play up your status as the underdog. And if Isaac underestimates you, so much the better."

"I'm so glad you're here. For everything," Alex said, gesturing around him to the house. "As if taking us in wasn't enough. Now you're donating your time and expertise to run my campaign. I can't thank you enough."

Maggie reached across the counter and squeezed his arm. "Let's get you elected before you thank me. And I've got a big investment in Rosemont. I don't want a bunch of idiots ruining Westbury and destroying my property value," she said with a smile.

Chapter 28

Susan had a mid-morning flight on Saturday and they set out for the airport after a quick breakfast. It was clear and sunny, the start of a spectacular day. They rode most of the way in companionable silence. Maggie finally turned to her daughter and asked, "Well, how are you feeling about things now?"

"You know, I can't believe how much stronger I feel. How much more peaceful. My relationship with Rob had gotten so dysfunctional. He was controlling; I was miserable. It happened so gradually that I didn't see it coming. I haven't missed him one bit."

"That's my girl! I'm so glad you came. I almost said 'home', but I don't know if you feel like Rosemont is home?" Maggie held her breath; her children might be grown, but she needed them to feel safe and at home with her.

"Rosemont is all that and more, for sure. It's just spectacular. I'm so excited that you get to live there. I can't wait to come back."

Maggie slowly exhaled. "So what's next for you? Any big cases you're working on?"

"There's always something. But I don't have any major deadlines until the fall. I may take a two-week trip to Europe. Would you like to come with me? Think about it." Maggie said she would. "And I still want to find Mr. Right," Susan said with a catch in her voice.

"You know what? I really feel you will. I'll bet that he's waiting for you right now. Rob has been tying up your attention. Now that you're free, the two of you will find each other. He may have been right in front of your nose all along but you've been too blind to see him."

"You really think so?"

"Absolutely. Things like that happen all the time."

"Well, maybe," Susan said.

"Open those beautiful eyes of yours and look around, ok?"

"I will, mom," Susan said with a bit more confidence.

They pulled off onto the airport exit. "When will you be in California on business again?"

"Not sure. With this election in eight weeks, I may not make a trip out until after that. I'll let you know."

"I have to hand it to you, mom, you're full of surprises. I can't wait to tell Mike that you are running a political campaign to unseat a corrupt mayor that you helped get indicted." She turned to scrutinize her mother. "Our mom is so cool."

They swung to the curbside check-in area. Susan dragged her luggage out of the back. Despite the dirty look from the police officer on duty, Maggie got out of the car and threw her arms around her daughter. "I love you and am so proud of you. I believe in your happy future, honey. No worries." She took Susan's now teary face in her hands and kissed her on both cheeks. The officer waved at them and shouted that Maggie needed to move her car. Susan smiled at her mom, picked up her luggage and set off.

Sam and Marc were setting up chairs in Fellowship Hall of the First Methodist Church while Beth made coffee in the kitchen. This would be Alex's initial campaign speech and he was nervously pacing in an adjacent Sunday school room.

"He's all set," Marc offered. "He's just got a case of the jitters. He'll be fine once he starts to speak. How many do you think will attend?"

"No idea," Sam answered. "We publicized this the best we could by email and word of mouth. We posted signs, too, but someone kept taking them down. People should start arriving any time now."

176

As they spoke, Council Member Chuck Delgado entered the room.

"Why, hello, boys. And lady," Delgado drawled. "You're expecting quite a crowd here, aren't you?" he said, looking at the Hall.

Beth, who had seen him enter the church from the kitchen window, spoke first. "We are. And that crowd will not include you. This meeting is for union members. It's not open to the general public. You need to turn around and head on out of here," she said in the authoritative tone of a seasoned schoolteacher.

"Now, Ms. O'Malley," Delgado replied. "Don't go gettin' all stirred up. I'm not here to make trouble. I just want to connect with the citizens during these troubled times. I want them to know I'm standing with them."

"Nonsense," Beth said. "You're here to spy for Russell Isaac. You should be ashamed of yourself." She was warming to the task of laying into him when the first attendees arrived. Sam signaled her to be quiet. She turned to offer coffee to the new arrivals while Delgado slipped into a seat on the far side of the room.

The room filled up fast and it was standing room only by the time Sam stepped to the front of the Hall and called the meeting to order. Delgado draped an arm casually across the seat back next to him and half-turned in his chair to face the door. His presence was noted. Two workers from Town Hall took one look at him and quickly exited. The Town Clerk, however, was not to be intimidated. She wove her way across the room to position herself directly behind him, turning the tables and keeping an eye on him instead of the other way around. Delgado snatched his arm from the back of the chair and shifted stiffly to the front. The Clerk patted her hair into place and settled her purse at her feet.

Sam cleared his throat and signaled for quiet. "I'm Sam Torres. Most of you know me. I work maintenance for the school system. I'm not a public speaker. My wife Joan works as a police dispatcher. We've been public employees our whole working lives. We've worked hard, paid all of our bills on time, and contributed to the pension plan. We've been counting on our pension and now that we're almost ready to retire, the money isn't there. Because someone stole it," he paused. "We can't let that stand. Our stewards have let us down," he said, looking pointedly

177

at Delgado. "We need new leadership at Town Hall. One of the brightest, most innovative and honest people I know is willing to step in to clean up this mess. He's going to speak to us for a few minutes and then we're going to ask you to sign petitions to get his name on the ballot. And if you'd be interested in working on his campaign, please see me or Beth." Sam straightened his shoulders and looked at the index card he was holding. "Alex Scanlon is an attorney and has his own firm here in town. Before that, he was a prosecutor. He was born and raised in Westbury. He was on the high school basketball team that won the state championship. He's raised money for the hospital and sits on the Library Advisory Board. Ladies and gentlemen: Alex Scanlon."

Thin applause rose from the crowd as Alex stepped to the front of the room. "Thank you for taking the time out of your busy Saturday to stop by. As Town employees, you've played a large part in making Westbury the place we know and love. A place where neighbors watch out for each other. If someone's dog gets lost, we drop everything and look for it. If we find a wallet on the street, we pick it up and return it to its rightful owner – with the money and credit cards intact. We sweep our sidewalks and mend our fences. We buy Girl Scout Cookies and candy bars for the sports teams. Our countryside is gorgeous, but this is a wonderful place to live and raise a family because of the people."

Heads nodded in agreement. Alex continued, "As you know, we've got widespread corruption in our Town government. Money is missing from the general fund and the pension fund. We don't yet know the full extent of the problem. Someone we trusted, our Mayor, is accused of betraying us. I don't know if he's guilty or not. That's up to the courts. And we don't know if anyone else was involved." People glanced surreptitiously at Delgado. He ignored the crowd and shot Alex a searing look. "We've all been victims of serious wrongdoing. My opponent Russell Isaac has not been indicted. But he's been on the Council for many years. If he didn't know about these problems, he should have. We don't need elected officials who aren't looking out for us. It took our new Council Member Tonya Holmes just a few short months to uncover the wrongdoing." All eyes were fixed on Alex.

"Mayor Wheeler's resignation gives us a chance to change course and get our finances back on firm footing and our Town headed into a prosperous and productive future. We all want Westbury to be a place where people are proud to work. We want our citizens to build meaningful careers and enjoy comfortable retirements right here. We're not going to be known as a seat of corruption. If I'm elected, we're going to clean up this mess. I won't allow us to be a laughing stock in the national press. We'll be a model of how ordinary people, like you and me, can take control and restore the ethics and decency that define a community." He paused as the crowd applauded.

"I'll need help from all of you to accomplish this. First, sign my petition and ask your friends and neighbors to sign. I need to get on the ballot. Second, turn out on Election Day to vote for me. And third, let me hear from you. I want your input as we define a new direction for our Town. No single person has all the answers. We need to clean up our finances and formulate a new Town General Plan. We need to address jobs, transportation, education, infrastructure, and public works. Together we can weather this storm and emerge more vibrant than ever. I'm betting on us," he concluded as he gestured to the crowd. Now applause swept the room.

A few people asked questions, but most were anxious to get on their way. Sam stood and announced that petitions were available by the entrance. Several people gathered around Alex with additional questions, while the remainder headed for the door. With the exception of Councilman Delgado, every person in attendance signed the petition. Delgado disappeared through a side exit.

Chapter 29

Maggie choked back tears as she pulled away from the airport and couldn't shake the low mood that shrouded her as she made the solitary drive back to Westbury. Since she planned to solicit signatures at the supermarket anyway, she decided to head straight there and collect them until two o'clock. Her goal was two hundred signatures.

The manager allowed her to set up her card table close to the entrance. Both his parents were Town retirees and he was one hundred percent behind her efforts. Shoppers were interested. Maggie was surprised that people wanted to stop and question her about Alex's plans to set the Town's finances on firm footing. Instead of sitting idle for most of the day, as she had feared, she spent the time in full campaign mode. The activity and lively conversations lifted her spirits, and by two o'clock she had one hundred and ninety-two signatures. Not one to abandon a goal, she continued until two-thirty, when she hit the two hundred mark.

Maggie stashed the table and petitions in her car and picked up a couple of nice steaks, some twice baked potatoes that she would only have to reheat, and the fixings for a good salad. She stopped at Laura's and picked up a pie for dessert. This wasn't the show-off, home-cooked meal she would have liked to serve John, but under the circumstances, it would have to do.

Maggie spent way more time getting ready than she had anticipated. Her hair was not cooperating and she noticed the spot on her blouse after she was fully dressed. Changing her blouse required a change in slacks and shoes – why were women's wardrobes so complicated? – and she was way behind schedule when she finally hit the kitchen. She realized that she had forgotten to pick up anything for an appetizer. She rummaged frantically through the refrigerator looking for some decent cheese, but came up empty-handed. So much for being an accomplished hostess, she chastised herself. She started the potatoes and was fixing the salad when John arrived. She leaned in and kissed him lightly. He was toting a bottle of wine and a bouquet of yellow tulips and presented them to her.

"These are lovely – tulips are my favorite. Did you know they continue to grow after they're cut? These will extend themselves another six inches and will bend along lovely arcs. So much fun to watch them do it. Thank you. Let's get these in water." She took his arm and led him to the kitchen. "Dinner is nothing fancy, I'm afraid. I spent most of the day at the supermarket, getting signatures. And I totally forgot about an appetizer, but the salad is almost ready, so if you're hungry we can start on it and then grill the steaks." She pulled out a vase and began cutting stems and arranging the flowers.

"No lunch today; I'm starved. The salad would be great. How about I open this?"

Maggie handed him a corkscrew and a couple of glasses. She dressed the salad and they took their plates to a small table on the patio that she had set for dinner. They leisurely chatted about the challenges of John's day. As she grilled the steaks, they inevitably turned to the topic of Alex's campaign.

"You're remarkable. You know that, don't you? I've never met anyone like you. You could be running for office. You have a total grasp of the issues and you know how to rally people to work toward a solution. You inspire confidence. I'd vote for you in a heartbeat," John said, holding Maggie's gaze.

Maggie flushed and looked away. "That's very kind, but I don't think so. People don't even know me around here. I think they're ready for a change, though. That was evident from the folks I talked to today. Alex has a good shot at this. I just hope that the opposition doesn't try something underhanded. I don't know if they're responsible for the fires, but I wouldn't be surprised."

"I agree," John replied. "It makes me nervous for you, too. You might be a target as his campaign manager."

Maggie turned to face him. "I've never heard of anybody's campaign staff being targeted. They always go for the candidate. But I'll be careful, don't you worry. I'm aware of my surroundings, I always lock my doors, and I faithfully set my alarm," she assured him as she picked up their empty plates. "It's getting chilly out here. Let's move inside."

Dessert started with pie-a-la mode on the sofa in the living room and progressed to old-fashioned necking. My God, this feels nice, Maggie thought. She was wondering how they could progress to the next level. How does one actually have a conversation about safe sex? Would he have come prepared with a condom? Do you get a blood test first? Why on earth hadn't she thought about all of this before now and asked someone? Who in the world did she know well enough to ask? Did John even want to? Ok, that was ridiculous, it was clear he wanted to.

They were interrupted by the alarm system announcing 'back kitchen door open.' Alex and Marc had just come home. Maggie and John shot up and began frantically straightening their clothes and smoothing their hair. Like a couple of teenagers, Maggie thought. The absurdity of the situation at this age and stage of their lives hit them and they couldn't suppress their guilty laughter, like altar boys in church. Alex and Marc entered the room and found them in a full-out fit of giggles.

They had seen John's car pulled up in front and had proceeded through the house slowly while making a lot of noise, so it was obvious that they had anticipated exactly what John and Maggie were doing. This realization only fueled their nervous laughter. Alex and Marc exchanged an uneasy glance.

Maggie pulled herself together and told Alex that her petitions from the afternoon were on the table in his room upstairs and he and Marc took the hint and quickly retired.

John took Maggie in his arm and held her tight. He leaned back and looked at her. "A close call, young lady. I didn't want to stop. I'm going to get a blood test. They'll give you a toll free number that you can call to get the results. Then we can get together at my place? I've only got dogs and cats living with me. Would that work?"

Maggie nodded her agreement, and told him she would do the same. John gave her another long, passionate kiss, and left her wondering how long it took to get the test results back.

Chapter 30

Sunday was a busy day for Alex's campaign as they circulated petitions at churches, real estate open houses, and in front of the Library. Sam and Joan swung by Rosemont in the late afternoon with one hundred and eighteen signatures. Tim arrived shortly after five with another fifty-two. Beth called on her way over with seventy-one. Maggie ran a tape and the grand total came to three thousand, five hundred and ninety-one signatures.

"We've done it," Alex announced to the small group of supporters. "Well, you've done it. We've got a comfortable margin here. I'll definitely get my name on the ballot. I can't thank you enough. You are the best friends anyone could ever hope for."

"We need to celebrate," Marc said. "Let's go get dinner at Pete's. My treat. I'll call Tonya and John to see if they can join us."

Tonya couldn't make it until dessert, but John was already at Pete's when they arrived. Pete ushered them into the private room upstairs. They recapped the events of the past few weeks and congratulated each other on bringing down the current administration. Pride and optimism marked their conversations as they worked their way through dinner toward dessert.

When Tonya arrived, John signaled for quiet and proposed a toast. "To our brave, hard-working elected officials, currently serving and soon-to-be elected. We appreciate your commitment and integrity. Godspeed as you meet the challenges before you. We're proud of you." John raised his glass. "To Tonya and Alex." The group followed suit and raised their glasses, amid a chorus of "Here, here."

Tonya rose. "To the best citizens one could hope to represent. To our beloved Westbury. And to our next mayor, Alex Scanlon." Once more, the group raised their glasses.

The conversation turned serious as Tim asked Alex about his campaign and the obstacles he anticipated. "We now need to get the word out. About the corruption at Town Hall and the need for new leadership. There are still people out there who don't know what's been going on. And we need to turn out the vote for me. We don't want anyone to feel that they can't make a difference."

Maggie added, "We'll file the petitions with the Town Clerk tomorrow. I'm going to get door hangers and mailers printed up right away. Alex will begin speaking whenever and wherever he can. If he isn't available, I'll speak on his behalf. The first 'meet the candidate' coffee at Rosemont will be next Sunday afternoon."

"What do you need help with?" Tim asked.

"We'll need people to distribute the door hangers. Talk with your neighbors and co-workers. Line up speaking engagements. Just let me know when and where you'd like him to appear. I'll keep the master calendar. Can we count on all of you?" she asked.

"Absolutely," Joan said, as Tim and Beth nodded.

"We're with you all the way," Sam added.

John checked his watch and reluctantly pushed his chair back. "I hate to break this up, but I have surgery at six in the morning."

"And we've all got a big day on the campaign trail tomorrow." Maggie observed. "Let's get a good night's sleep and get cracking first thing."

Chapter 31

The next seven weeks flew by in a blur of activity. Everyone in attendance at Pete's that night was as good as his or her word. Literature was distributed. Signs were posted in every yard. Alex was in and out of living rooms, church basements, school cafeterias, and even parking lots every single night; meeting citizens, listening to their concerns, and outlining solutions. He was even busier on the weekends. Maggie acted as his stand-in and spoke almost as often as he did.

With the short campaign season, they didn't want to turn down any opportunity to reach voters, no matter how small. Maggie was so busy that the hoped-for cozy evening with John didn't materialize. They both managed to get the all-clear on their blood tests, which fueled their fire to get together. They just couldn't find the time. Instead, they texted during the day and talked on the phone every night, usually in the wee hours, rehashing the events of the day and the challenges ahead. John attended all of the Sunday afternoon "meet the candidate" coffees at Rosemont. And through all of this, Maggie managed to keep her consulting practice going and her clients happy. She was at once exhausted by the constant rushing around and exhilarated by the warm response she unfailingly received from everyone she addressed.

During one such busy Sunday afternoon, Frank Haynes set out for the freeway and instead of getting into the eastbound lane that would take him home, he headed west. Like a stalker seeking his prey, he was fixated on Rosemont. He accelerated as he entered the freeway and opened his moon roof so that the air rushed pleasantly around his ears. A perverse smile spread across his brittle lips. Maybe losing this election would sour her on Westbury and prompt her to sell Rosemont.

Exhilarated, he settled comfortably into his leather seat and tuned into the business news. Before long, he was slipping his car into his usual spot in the wide berm on the road below Rosemont; the same spot where he had observed the carnival set-up. It afforded a good view of most of the backyard and one side of Rosemont. He couldn't see anyone in the yard. Windows on the first floor were lit, but he couldn't make out any detail with his unaided eye. He reached into his glove box and retrieved the expensive binoculars he bought recently from that insufferable salesclerk who actually believed that he wanted them for bird watching.

The binoculars were excellent for his purpose. He finally located a group of four people in what appeared to be a living room. He recognized Maggie, the fag Scanlon, and two other men he couldn't identify. One of them might have been that realtor, Knudsen, but he couldn't be sure. Maggie was on the move, pointing to a flipchart. One of the men rose to retrieve a stack of papers. Try as he might, he couldn't read anything on the flipchart. They're working it, that's for sure, he silently cursed. And working it hard. This isn't a whim on Scanlon's part. He's out to win this election. I need to find out if they're gaining ground on Isaac.

Haynes swung his car onto the roadway as he punched a number on his speed dial. The recipient picked up right away. "I've got another job for you," Haynes barked before the other party could utter a word.

The man slipped unobtrusively into the back of the crowd as candidate Scanlon was introduced to the small group of retired veterans assembled at the VFW hall. Scanlon presented a compelling presentation of the suspected problems with the Town's finances and his suggested solutions, highlighting his experience as a prosecutor. The crowd was resonating with him.

Maggie leaned against a wall, off to one side, satisfied with the proceedings.

The question and answer session showed Scanlon to be even more effective off-the-cuff. By the end, he was generating spontaneous applause to almost every answer. To a person, the crowd was hooked on each word he said. No doubt about it, Scanlon had charisma. His opponent may have seriously underestimated Alex Scanlon. It looked like this election would be a real horse race.

The man exited quietly. He wasn't looking forward to being the bearer of bad news to Frank Haynes, but it had to be done. He pulled out his phone and dialed the familiar number.

Frank Haynes was, predictably, not pleased with the report on candidate Scanlon's successful outing at the VFW Hall. This was supposed to be a cakewalk for Isaac. He was an incumbent, for God's sake. The last thing they needed was to have an ex-prosecutor in the Mayoral seat, poking into things. Shit!

He pushed his chair back abruptly from his desk and began to pace. The VFW was just one appearance, but judging by the number of Scanlon signs popping up in storefronts and on lawns all over town, Scanlon's campaign was gaining momentum. He raked his hands through his well-manicured hair. They had to do something to stop him. Fast. And he couldn't look for help from Delgado and his goons. The fires were still being investigated.

He'd already had Scanlon investigated for past indiscretions and come up empty-handed. The prick was a fucking saint. Haynes tore off his tie and shoved it in his open briefcase. The idea hit him on his last lap around his desk. Get rid of Maggie Martin. Or at least neutralize her. Have Isaac meet with her like she had been pestering him to do since their conversation at the restaurant. Listen to all of her questions and ideas. Praise her for her insight and hard work. Flatter her by agreeing to appoint her to Isaac's open Council seat when he was elected Mayor. Convince her that she could put her time and talents to good use for the Town after the election was over. They'd announce that she was part of their team to revitalize Westbury.

Haynes settled back into his chair and breathed deeply. It was a brilliant plan. When there was something in it for them, people usually gave up their allegiances and threw in with their self-interests. Hell, if she told Scanlon, he'd probably encourage her to take them up on their offer. And she wouldn't be able to work on his campaign anymore. That might just slow Scanlon down enough to allow Isaac to win.

He rested his chin on steepled fingers. They wouldn't actually appoint her to the Council, of course. They'd come up with some plausible reason – most likely her short tenure in Westbury. And that might tick her off enough to send her packing, with him waiting in the wings with a low-ball offer for Rosemont. With a smirk plastered firmly on his lips, he walked out to his secretary and directed her to get Russell Isaac on the phone.

Maggie absent-mindedly fidgeted with the cap of the water bottle the clerk had given her while she waited for Russell Isaac to finish up whatever business he was attending to down the hall. She was in a windowless office in the back of his auto parts store. Maggie turned anxiously as footsteps approached, only to be disappointed when they passed on by. She had a million things to do and was fuming at the rudeness of being called to this meeting and then kept waiting. I ought to get up and leave, she thought – all the while knowing that she would do no such thing. Maggie had been surprised when she received Isaac's call, inviting her to meet with him. After all of her unreturned phone calls to him, she had given up. And, now, here she was. Alex was probably right – Isaac had an ulterior motive. Well, she would be ready for him. He wasn't going to trap her into revealing anything.

Her reverie was interrupted as Frank Haynes strode into the room, hand outstretched and a smile arranged on his face. "Maggie, how are you?" he said as she stood and they shook hands. "No, please – sit. How's that dog of yours?"

"She's just fine, Frank. Thank you for asking. But you didn't invite me here to talk about dogs. Where's Acting Mayor Isaac?"

"Some auto-parts emergency, no doubt. He's finishing up – in fact, that's him coming down the hall now."

"So sorry to keep you waiting, my dear," Isaac patronized as he entered the room. Maggie's spine stiffened. This time, she didn't get up. Flustered, Isaac turned to Haynes. "Hello, Frank." He clumsily made his way to the chair behind the desk.

Maggie remained silent and looked pointedly at each man in turn.

Isaac cleared his throat. "I was sincere when I told you a few weeks ago that I still represent you and want to know what your concerns and issues are." He paused and waited expectantly for her to respond.

Maggie simply smiled and shrugged. "You've heard our platform; you should be very familiar with our issues by now."

"Well, yes, on the surface. We wanted to invite you here to share your concerns with us in depth."

"Why thank you," Maggie replied sweetly, "but I really don't have anything to add. Maybe you can tell me what you intend to do about the rampant financial mismanagement that's occurred on your watch?"

Isaac scowled and began turning his wedding ring around on his finger. He's at a loss for words, Maggie realized with satisfaction.

Haynes interjected. "That's all part of an ongoing criminal investigation. We really can't formulate any plans until that's completed," he stated calmly. "But we have another, more important reason for inviting you here today." He looked at Isaac, who gestured for Haynes to continue.

"Your commitment to the community and knowledge of the issues has not gone unnoticed. We're all quite impressed with you." He paused and Isaac nodded in agreement. "When Russell is elected Mayor…"

"If he's elected Mayor," Maggie interjected.

Haynes struggled to conceal his irritation. He continued, "We'd like to appoint you to fill his Council seat. You'd be a great asset to this Town."

A hardness set in around Maggie's eyes. These pompous fools thought she would be so flattered that she would jump at their offer – would leave Alex and his campaign in the dust. Probably because that's what they would do in the same situation, she surmised.

She leaned forward in her chair and paused until Isaac quit fiddling with his ring and Haynes was staring at her. "Hear this, gentlemen. Under no circumstances would I entertain such an offer. I am not a politician and don't aspire to political office. And more importantly, your bringing me in here now and making this offer is most inappropriate. You're trying to bribe me to leave Alex's campaign. That's despicable."

Isaac's face reddened and his nostrils flared. "Watch yourself," he sputtered. Before he could continue, Haynes interrupted. "That's not what we meant, Maggie. You misunderstood. You can continue to work on Alex's campaign if that's what you want to do. We just hope you will consider joining us on the Town Council if Russell's spot opens up. That's all we meant. Don't go misconstruing this," he concluded.

"I know what you intended." She straightened her shoulders and rose deliberately, turning to face them. My refusal has caught them completely off guard, she realized. Sensing an advantage, she pressed on. "While I'm here, why don't we schedule that candidate's debate we've been requesting? I really don't think you can refuse me now." Maggie fixed them with a steely stare.

"Of course. We've been meaning to get back to you; we've had trouble finding a venue." Haynes' tone was conciliatory.

"I've reserved Haynes Gymnasium for the Thursday night before the election," Maggie replied, and was pleased to note the tick by Haynes' right eye. "We're set; I'll alert the press. See you both then."

Frank Haynes pulled into the lot behind the liquor store and got wearily out of his car. God, he was sick of these meetings in the middle of the night. When this is over, I'll never get involved with these bottom-feeders again. If this is ever over. He took a deep breath and steadied himself. He knew it would do no good to unleash his fury on this drunken fool. He waited for the familiar buzz, mounted the steps, and slowly entered Delgado's office.

"How ya doin', Frankie boy?" Delgado slurred.

"I'm in better shape than you are, Chuck. That's obvious."

"Depends on your point of view, there, Frankie. Have a drink," he said as he slid the open bottle across the desk toward Haynes. "Do you good to lighten up."

"I'm not feeling too lighthearted these days. Neither should you. Did Isaac tell you about the mess he made trying to offer that Martin bitch his Council seat if he wins?"

"He said she didn't want it, yeah. That broad's not important. Quit getting yourself all bunched up over her. We're still going to win the election."

"How do you figure that? Scanlon's got all the momentum. If Isaac doesn't clean up at the debate, we're finished. Of all the people we don't want as Mayor, Scanlon is at the top of the list."

"The debate won't matter much, Frankie. I've got plans for Scanlon. If it goes bad. We're all set."

"Like the fires? Some shit-for-brains plan like that?" Haynes spat. His jaw tightened and he clenched his right fist. "What the fuck is wrong with you guys? We're all under the microscope here. There's no room for error. Not anymore."

"Know what your problem is, Frankie? You got no balls. Get the hell outta here and let me get back to work," Delgado said as he reached for his bottle.

"Don't fuck this up, Delgado. I'm warning you," Haynes seethed. He tripped and caught himself, cursing, as he stormed down the stairs.

When set up theater-style, the gymnasium held six hundred. Reporters from papers all over the state were present, as were two television crews. The scandal of the Mayor's resignation in the wake of his corruption indictment focused more attention on the election of this small-town mayor than would normally be warranted. The gym was filled to capacity thirty minutes before the scheduled start of the debate.

Alex and Maggie arrived an hour early and were rehearsing in the locker room, going over talking points and anticipating questions. Neither one wanted to acknowledge it, but they were both anxious and a bit scared. The moderator was the Head Librarian, a good choice. He was a distinguished-looking man in his sixties who had held that post longer than anyone could remember and had probably "shushed" every person in attendance at one time or another for talking in the Library. He would keep control of the crowd and would make both candidates observe the time limits and stick to the rules. The list of questions had been prepared by the local chapter of the Daughters of the American Revolution.

Maggie was adjusting Alex's tie for the umpteenth time when they got the call to enter the gym. She leaned in and whispered, "You are perfectly prepared. I believe in you completely. Just stay on message, no matter what Isaac says or does," she admonished sternly. They stepped through the double doors by the stage and into the gaudy light of the gymnasium.

It took a few minutes for the crowd to realize that the candidates were on stage and it was time to start. Maggie fought her way to the seat that John and Marc had saved for her in the front row. The moderator called for quiet, led the crowd in the Pledge of Allegiance, and introduced both candidates. He outlined the rules of the debate and started off by directing the first question to Isaac.

It was clear that Isaac was well prepared. Gone was the awkward bumbler who had accepted the post of Acting Mayor only a few short weeks ago. He was expensively dressed and well groomed. His style was self-deprecating and charming. He's got charisma, Maggie hated to admit. His themes were to distance himself from Wheeler, stress his experience on the Council, and his success as a businessman. He elicited the occasional laugh and polite applause.

Alex's first answer was overly complicated. The crowd grew bored and inattentive. He's getting lost in the minutia, Maggie thought. He sought out Maggie in the crowd when he finished his first answer, which had been greeted with tepid applause. In exaggerated fashion, she mouthed the words, "TOO MUCH DETAIL." He shook his head in recognition.

As the evening progressed, Alex picked up steam. He simplified his answers and was bolstered by the growing enthusiasm of the crowd's response. Isaac, in contrast, was losing ground. The initial appeal of his mannerisms and message was growing stale.

When the last question had been answered and the candidates shook hands to signal the end of the debate, it was apparent that the audience favored Alex by a wide margin. He was inundated by people swarming to the front to shake his hand. Other than a few followers in attendance, no one bothered to approach Isaac. Maggie thought that he looked dumbstruck by this turn of events. "He hasn't taken Alex seriously at all," Maggie observed to John. "Look at him. He's a deer in the headlights. I don't think it ever dawned on him until now that he could lose this election."

Maggie and John hung back until the last well-wisher departed. Marc was clapping Alex on the back and enthusing about every aspect of his performance as Maggie sidled over to them. Alex smiled wide enough to turn himself inside out. He swept her into a hug that lifted her off her feet. John pumped his hand, "You nailed it. Well done."

"Did you get a look at Isaac? He must feel like he's been run over by a steamroller. He didn't expect this in a million years." Marc laughed.

"Tonight was a nice moment, I'll have to admit. A high point. I knew I got off to a bad start, by the way. Thanks for the coaching," he nodded at Maggie. "We'll see how this turns out on Tuesday. We're almost there. I'm encouraged. I've been pretty exhausted, but this was like pouring jet fuel on me. I'm ready to keep going."

"Me too. Exactly how I feel," Maggie replied.

They ambled out to the deserted parking lot, reluctant to leave the scene of their success. "Marc and I need to stop by my office on the way home to sign paperwork for the insurance company. It'll only take a minute, if you don't mind," he said to Maggie. Before she could answer, John offered to take her home and Maggie readily accepted.

They were following Marc and Alex on the two-lane road through the woods back into town when it happened. A log obstructed the road just as it curved to the left. If it hadn't been such a dark night, and if they had been driving slower, they might have been able to avoid it. As it was, they barely had time to apply

194

the brakes before the devastating impact. The vehicle skidded, impacted the log full on, and rolled over twice before coming to a stop on the far side of the road.

Maggie and John were only seconds behind. They heard the terrible crash before they came upon it. Maggie had her cell phone out and was dialing 911 as John screeched to a stop next to the vehicle. He slammed his car into park and flew out the door, shouting to Maggie to get his flashlight out of the glove box.

Alex's door was jammed shut but John managed to pry the rear passenger door open. Maggie shined the flashlight into the vehicle and fear pierced her like an ax. Blood was splattered everywhere. Both men had been wearing seat belts and the air bags had deployed.

Alex began to moan softly. He had a large gash over one eye and his nose was strangely angled to the right. Marc started to come to. He began to flail agitatedly at his seat belt and John reached over the back seat to restrain him, telling him that he had been in an accident and help was on the way. Why on earth are they taking so long, Maggie thought.

John concentrated on keeping Marc calm. Alex never stirred, but his breathing was regular. After what seemed like an eternity, they heard the siren of the approaching ambulance. Maggie stepped away as the EMT's took over. John climbed out of the back seat and joined her. They watched in anxious silence as Marc was quickly placed on a stretcher and taken away. A second ambulance arrived and waited, lights flashing in the otherwise still night, while the paramedics labored to extricate Alex from the vehicle.

A police cruiser pulled up next and a uniformed officer spoke to one of the paramedics, who pointed to Maggie and John. The officer exchanged a few more words with the paramedic and joined them at the side of the road. "I'm Officer Jackson. Did you see the accident?"

"No," John replied. "We were following them and came on the scene maybe twenty seconds afterwards. We heard the crash."

"Which direction were you heading?"

"North. Both cars were heading north. The driver, Alex Scanlon, is the mayoral candidate. Maggie is his campaign manager. We were all returning home from the candidate's debate at the gym earlier this evening."

"Did you see any other vehicles in the vicinity?" John shook his head.

"Any people hanging around? Watching? Anyone else offer to help that isn't here now?"

"No. No one."

"Any idea where that log came from?"

"None. That's what we were wondering. How in the world did that log get in the middle of the road?"

Officer Jackson shook his head. They turned as the paramedics removed Alex from the vehicle. He was now in a neck brace and was being strapped to a gurney.

"Can I go with him?" Maggie asked. "Will they let me ride to the hospital with him?"

"I'll find out for you," the Officer said. "At the very least, we can find out where they're taking him."

The paramedics refused Maggie's request but said that Alex was stable and they were talking him to Westbury Memorial Hospital. As the ambulance started its siren and sped off, Officer Jackson took down their contact information and waved them off in the direction of the hospital.

Maggie scrolled through her contact list and called, one after the other, Tonya, Sam, Beth, Pete and Tim. By the time they parked and got into the emergency room waiting area, they were told that Marc was in stable condition and had been admitted for a broken collarbone and wrist, and that Alex was in X-Ray. They got cups of coffee from a vending machine, more for something to do than with any desire for coffee. They were alternately pacing and nursing their drinks when Sam and Joan came through the automatic doors, with Tim on their heels.

"Oh my God," Joan cried. "I can't believe this. How are they?"

Maggie brought them up to speed with what little information she had. Tonya joined them as a nurse approached the group. We've got a small private waiting room for families. I'm going to put you in there. You'll be more comfortable. They've just taken Alex to surgery."

"What are they operating on?" John asked.

"The surgeon will talk to you as soon as she's done. That's all I can tell you for now."

"Can anyone go see the other man in the crash? He's been admitted. Someone should be with him," Maggie said.

"I think that'll be fine," she said. "I'll find out what room he's in for you."

By the time the nurse got back to them, Pete had arrived and they decided that he should stay with Marc. They would call him on his cell phone as soon as they heard anything about Alex. Two-and-a-half endless hours later a tired-looking woman in surgical dress introduced herself as Dr. Mertz.

"You're Alex Scanlon's family and friends?" They all nodded. "He's suffered traumatic injuries to his pelvis and fractured bones in both legs. He has three cracked ribs and a broken nose. And he suffered a deep cut over his right eye. But none of his internal organs were compromised and his vital signs are stable. We operated to replace his hip and inserted pins in both of his legs. We stitched his cut and realigned his nose. The ribs will heal on their own. He's in recovery and hasn't regained consciousness. We'll keep him heavily sedated for the next day or two. He may need additional surgeries and will certainly require months of physical therapy, but he's young and healthy and we expect him to make a full recovery. He's been very fortunate.

The group let out a collective sigh. "Can we see him?" Joan asked.

"No," the doctor replied. "He's resting comfortably and we'll keep him in ICU tonight and at least all day tomorrow. One or two of you can see him then. He won't be up to visits from all of you. The most helpful thing you can do for him now is go home and get some sleep."

The relieved and exhausted group, left with no other choice, relayed the news to Pete and headed home to salvage as much sleep from the remainder of the night as possible. John asked Maggie if she was afraid to stay at Rosemont by herself. "If you want company, I'm happy to sleep on the sofa. Tonight isn't the romantic evening I have planned for us," he said with a rueful smile. Maggie assured him that was not necessary and she would be fine, but that had been a lie. She was deeply disturbed by what she had seen in that car and by the implications for Alex and, frankly, all of them. It was obvious to her that he would not be physically capable of serving as Mayor for months or possibly years. And she was convinced that the sudden appearance of the log had a sinister explanation. Like the fires.

She dozed intermittently until she couldn't force herself to stay in bed any longer. She got up, tended to Eve, quickly showered and dressed and was back at the hospital by six-thirty. She wanted to catch the doctors on their morning rounds. Alex lay still and flat in his shadowy room, lit only by the monitors he was hooked up to. He looked peaceful and the lines squiggling across the monitors were all consistent and steady. She pulled up a chair and took one of his hands. She thought he tried to squeeze hers, but couldn't be sure.

Maggie spent the day at the hospital, talking to doctors and nurses, and forwarding information to Marc. She called Susan, who had been shocked and disturbed by the news. Maggie insisted she didn't need to take emergency leave to come out, but if she could schedule a trip over a long weekend, that would be helpful. The doctors reduced Alex's narcotic IV in mid-afternoon, and by four o'clock he came around. He recognized Maggie, asked about Marc, and whispered that he was in pain. The nurse restored his IV to prior levels and he floated back to dreamland.

Maggie, exhausted from the day of leafing through magazines she couldn't focus on and trying to eat food she had no appetite for, headed home. She intended to turn on the TV and check her email. She fed Eve and sat down for just a minute to collect her thoughts. She leaned back in the library chair that had become her refuge since that first night at Rosemont. The next time she looked at her watch, it was two in the morning. She fought the urge to go right back to sleep where she was and forced herself upstairs and into bed.

The next two days followed the same routine. Alex was making steady progress and was spending longer periods awake.

He was now eating a soft diet. They had moved him out of ICU and put him on the same floor as Marc. Alex would go to inpatient rehab for several weeks after he left the hospital. Marc was scheduled to come home to Rosemont.

Tonya and Tim intercepted her at the hospital on Sunday. They confirmed that Alex's accident had been front-page, top-of-the-hour news. Isaac's people had wasted no time in planting the idea that Alex would not be fit to serve as Mayor given his tragic accident and grievous injuries.

Maggie agreed that he would not be able to serve and, although she hated the injustice of the situation, she didn't see any other course of action but to let them have the election. She didn't have the time or energy to pursue an alternative if she had seen one.

Tonya made a cryptic mention of having a Plan B and tried to elaborate, but Maggie spotted Dr. Mertz heading down the corridor to Alex's room. She was intent on having a word with the doctor and bid a hasty goodbye to Tonya and Tim, tossing over her shoulder that anything they wanted to do was fine with her. She trusted them to do the right thing.

Chapter 32

Maggie fully expected they would put out a gracious press release, thanking everyone for their support of Alex's campaign and for their prayers and well wishes. She didn't think any more about it. And she was most certainly not prepared for what happened next.

When Election Day rolled around that Tuesday, Maggie was so busy helping Marc get in and out of bed and arranging for Alex's transfer to rehab, that she didn't even vote. Why bother? Russell Isaac had won this round by default and, frankly, it made her sick to think about it.

If Maggie had gone to the polls, she would have been amazed to see the volunteers at each and every polling place, from the time they opened to the time they closed, stationed at the required distance, soliciting votes for a write-in candidate. A newcomer to Town who seemed like she had been part of this community her whole life. The dynamic spirit behind the successful Easter carnival. The energetic soul who was willing to get creative and roll up her sleeves to pitch in and help others. The new voice and breath of fresh air that this Town needed. A successful business owner and forensic accountant with the experience and expertise they needed to lead Westbury forward. MAGGIE MARTIN. Write her into our future!

Frank Haynes retired early on election night. The tension of the past few weeks had taken its toll. It was all finally over and he felt certain that Isaac was a shoe-in. He hated to admit it, but that accident that Delgado arranged worked like a charm. Voters wanted someone capable of being firmly at the helm in the Mayor's Office. Hell – that's the drum that Scanlon's own campaign had been beating. What did they call that? Being hoist on your own petard? He kept his ear to the ground, but so far there wasn't any talk about that tree trunk being other than an unfortunate obstruction on the highway. Haynes settled back into his pillows as he patted the mattress and his faithful border collie jumped up to join him.

Haynes woke at his usual time the next morning. He was in no hurry as he let the dog out, fixed her breakfast, and made his coffee. He picked the newspaper off his front step and proceeded to his bedroom to shower and dress. He flipped it open and the headline assaulted him as he slumped onto the edge of his bed. Good God Almighty, what were they going to do now?"

WRITE IN CANDIDATE MAGGIE MARTIN ELECTED MAYOR
Major Upset After Debilitating Injury of Candidate Alex Scanlon
First Write-In Mayor in State's History

When she retrieved her newspaper on Wednesday morning, Maggie also gasped as she read the headline. Her world spun around her as she stood rooted to her front porch, paper in hand. She widened her stance to steady herself. How the hell had they done this to her, without asking her? But even as she thought this, a wave of excitement washed over her and a smile broke forth, scattering her doubts and fears. I can do this. I really truly can do this. She squared her shoulders and set her gaze above the trees. Why not? I can figure out what to do here. With the help and grace of God, I can make a difference. If all of these good people believe in me, then I ought to believe in myself. I will not let them down.

She resolutely crossed her threshold, and when the massive front door of Rosemont closed on her this time, the tentative woman looking for a fresh start was gone, replaced by the new Mayor of Westbury.

"Well, Eve, looks like we've got a Town to run," she said as she tossed the paper aside. "We'd better get cracking. This is the start of my next chapter." She turned and raced up the stairs, with Eve bounding happily at her heels.

#######

About the Author

Barbara Hinske is a practicing attorney who inherited the fiction-writing gene from her father. She began her career as an industrial engineer, but found her true passion in the law. She has two children – now grown – with her exceedingly kind and good second husband, who died of cancer in 2006. Lucky in love, Barb married another exceptional man and father of two in 2010, and they live in Phoenix, Arizona, in their own Rosemont, with their two adorable and spoiled dogs.

Coming to Rosemont is the first book in the *Rosemont* series.

You can learn more by visiting her website at www.barbarahinske.com.

Follow her on twitter at @BHinske.

Facebook at http://on.fb.me/VAzlmi

See photos of the fictional Rosemont, Westbury, and things related to the book at www.pinterest.com/barbarahinske.

35717302R00124

Made in the USA
Charleston, SC
16 November 2014